ISBN: 1500868531
ISBN-13: 978-1500868536

FICTION / General
FICTION / Coming of Age
FICTION / Fantasy / Urban
FICTION / Gothic
FICTION / Political
FICTION / Romance / General
FICTION / Romance / New Adult
FICTION / Romance / Paranormal
FICTION / Thrillers / Supernatural
FICTION / Thrillers / Political

After the Vampire's Gala

"HOW CAN I WANT YOU?" I didn't realize I had said the words aloud until they reached my own ears. "God, this bond—it's crazy."

"You may look upon what we have in horror, but how do you think we regard your human relationships? Your affections wax and wane." Contempt dripped from every word even as he trailed his hand down my neck and across my shoulder and arm, his touch sending shards of desire through me as he seemed to drink me with his eyes. "You marry for love but also for convenience, from tradition, for stability and companionship, for money, for children, or simply because people expect it of you."

I swayed in the force of his regard, but I couldn't deny what he said.

He continued, "And what you feel on your wedding night and what you feel five years later, ten, twenty, forty—even true love may not last, or it may blossom and fade several times over. We are as constant as the sun. Our hearts are not our own to give, but once they are taken, they do not—they cannot—waver." He reached my hand and took it, clasping it in his own.

Another jolt went straight through my body even as my mind rebelled at his words. He was equating a bond—our bond—with love, but there was nothing that I had seen that night that was anything like the kind of love I believed in.

Aethereal Bonds

aetherealbonds.com

DEDICATION

To Tricia.

CONTENTS

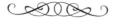

CHAPTER ONE

*"I*t is my honor to present Dorian Thorne and Cora Shaw.*"*

The words were soft but resonant, filling the room from hidden speakers to announce my arrival on Dorian's arm. The hum of the crowd dropped into silence.

My eyes were fixed straight ahead as we took the last few steps down to the balcony landing, where the single flight of stairs split into halves that doubled back to continue down on either side.

I didn't want to run. Not anymore. Dorian had taken that desire from me, and in the process, he'd shown me that he could take everything. He'd proven that I belonged to him, utterly and completely, and any faint resistance I could mount against him was only at his whim.

At least, I thought bitterly, he allowed me to still feel my fear.

I'd avoided looking over the railing into the grand salon as we descended the first flight of stairs—I had that much choice left to me—but as we turned on the landing, I had to face the room and the guests who were gathered below, waiting to meet me.

My hand tightened convulsively around Dorian's arm.

Hundreds of faces were turned to look up at us, eyes glittering, lips red gashes that were parted in smiles of varying shades of sincerity. The impression of falseness was overpowering. They looked human, but their appearances were so calculated to hit every note of physical beauty that they seemed like a gallery of mannequins that had been given life.

They were vampires—or agnates, as they called themselves—and a few of their not-quite-human consorts. And at least one of them wanted me dead.

"There are so many," I whispered, freezing on the top step. I couldn't force my legs to move.

"It's a special occasion," Dorian murmured. "Every agnate who could come is here, from hundreds or even thousands of miles away."

I looked up at him. His tone was almost conspiratorial, like that of one outsider to another. But he was one of them. He looked like one of them, moved like one of them, with his aristocratic features under his dark, waving hair. He even smiled like one of them right then, a reflex that didn't reach his eyes, a public face meant for the benefit of the assembly below.

And yet I craved him every bit as much as I feared the others. It was an ache in my bones, a hole in my chest, a sense of a phantom missing limb that was only eased when his touch sent electric awareness coursing through my body to bring me to life.

His children, I reminded myself. That feeling was a trap to make me want to bear his children and make more creatures like those below. And the very thought made me want to scream.

But I didn't, because only a short time ago, it had also made me want to run away. Then he'd plucked that desire right out of my mind while I stood there, helpless to stop him. So even though my head spun and my breath dragged inside my lungs, I didn't dare to even protest out of the fear of what else he'd take from me.

The guests applauded at our appearance, a polite and restrained sound that was pitched to be continued for minutes without flagging. Dorian put his free hand over mine where it creased the sleeve of his tail coat.

"Come on, now," he said, his blue eyes capturing me. "We shouldn't leave them waiting."

There was something in his expression that I'd never seen before. Victory. Exhilaration. Was it me that caused these new emotions? No—no, it was only what I meant to his cause in the role of his consort, his cognate.

He took the next step, and I came with him even though my heart felt so tight I thought it would choke me. I would follow him to hell because I had to. My feet wobbled in their heels.

A blast of trumpets accompanied our advance, the opening to an exultant processional played by the chamber orchestra perching upon the far end of the mezzanine above the salon. And the clapping continued as we reached the edge of the red carpet that ran from the foot of the stairs to the center of the room.

The dazzling assembly swirled before my eyes, as if Tim Burton had been set loose on the Academy Awards. Couture fought with costumes that must have been centuries old, hoop skirts and Louboutins, knee breeches and Armani. Rubies battled lamé, diamonds clashed with sequins, and feather boas rivaled stuffed foxes, all thrown together with a mad abandon that crashed in my senses.

The guests melted away on either side as we followed the strip of carpet. I risked a look over my shoulder. The crowd closed up behind us as soon as we passed.

Surrounded. Trapped. My heart skittered madly out of control. If I had been able to run then, I would have.

The carpet ended at the foot of a towering, black-draped object in the exact center of the vast room. Dorian came to a stop in front of it, and he turned us around to face the crowd just as the orchestra let out one last chord and fell into silence, the applause dying with it.

He had timed our arrival with theatrical precision, making the most of the moment. And I was the prop, swaying on his arm.

"Today marks two beginnings." Dorian's voice

rolled out over the assembly. His face was perfectly composed, but I could see the cold flash of triumph in his eyes as he looked across his friends and enemies. "One is personal, the beginning of my bond to my new cognate, Cora Shaw. The other is a new beginning for us all, because I found Cora not in the old way but through the new reproducible, scientific screening techniques developed by the research that I and my compatriots have been funding these last thirty years."

Applause erupted again, this time far louder, though it came from fewer hands. Some agnates didn't clap at all, and some of the fake smiles turned into something that more closely resembled snarls. I could feel all the eyes on me like a weight—a sense of hope from some, hate from others.

I shuddered away from all of them. I was just...myself. Not a symbol. Not a tool. I hadn't chosen this dubious honor, and I didn't deserve the burden of their emotions.

Agnates like Dorian had to feed on blood from a living human to survive, but only one human in thousands would normally survive the feeding—and in the process be transformed into an ageless cognate, bonded to the vampire who bit them and able to provide blood as needed forever after. Dorian's tests screened out those who couldn't be turned, improving those odds to one in one hundred.

An ordinary college student, I'd been dying from leukemia. The transformation cured human illnesses, so when Dorian's tests revealed that I was an excellent candidate, I'd taken the chance—without knowing that he was offering more than a cancer treatment. Without knowing the nature of the change until it was far too late.

I wished I could hate Dorian for it, but any time I reached for such an emotion, it slithered away, out of my grasp.

A noise and a sudden breeze behind us made me look back. The drape was falling away from the tall object, revealing a black marble sculpture more than twice life size—a nude winged man surging up from the base, wings extended and arm uplifted as he rose, his face turned up to the ceiling far overhead.

Dorian continued, speaking over the applause. "In commemoration of this historic event, I commissioned a work, Angel Rising. Let it be a representation of the new age that we are about to enter."

The angry muttering rose in volume, but other agnates clapped louder, some even cheering in support.

"Bravo! Bravo!" called a soprano voice, and I saw Clarissa, one of Dorian's friends, deep in the crowd with her hands cupped around her mouth.

Dorian held up a hand, and gradually, the noise died away. "And now let us observe the venerable institution of the introduction of a new cognate in the spirit of harmony with which it is traditionally kept."

Applause again, quieter, and this time, there were expressions of naked outrage on some of the agnates' faces.

The orchestra struck up a spritely classical piece. As if that were some kind of a signal, the crowd shifted, the bubble of space around us collapsing as the agnates turned their attention to each other.

"I only caught about half of that, but I think you just made a whole bunch of really dangerous vampires really mad," I whispered.

"We've won," Dorian said, contempt naked in his voice. "Those who don't accept that will be passed by."

"Well, one of *those* has already sent an assassin after me," I reminded him. They had wanted to erase the evidence of my existence before I could be presented to vampire society. "Making them angrier doesn't really seem like a healthy choice."

He glanced down at me, and something shifted behind his eyes, like he was really looking at me for the first time. His face softened instantly. "I know you're afraid, Cora. But you're untouchable now. The introduction makes you as safe as you can be. It's been centuries since an agnate harmed another's officially recognized cognate."

I looked over the glittering crowd, wondering which of them might choose to make an exception. In contrast to their opponents, Dorian and his allies believed that agnates should not exploit humans indiscriminately. But to restrain their feeding had meant drastically reducing the chances of finding a cognate. Now Dorian's research changed all that. And that made his enemies hate me, the living proof.

"Let's not test that," I said. "What happens next?"

"Next?" Dorian nodded at the company. "Next we greet those of our guests who wish to congratulate me or be introduced to you."

As if summoned by his words, a silver-haired man

headed straight for us, an ethereal woman clad in diaphanous nude draperies drifting behind him. He was one of the few vampires who wore obvious signs of age— but they seemed to be just that, worn, like I might wear a coat.

"Very subtle, Dorian." The man nodded toward the statue. "Maybe you should put sparklers on it, or a loudspeaker. Truly drive home your point. Someone might have missed it."

"Like it, do you?" Dorian said. There was a small, smug lift at the corner of his mouth.

"Others don't," the man said dryly. "How long have you had it sitting in storage, waiting for this day?"

"Thirty-four years."

"You know that some will say it is just luck," he said.

Dorian's gaze went icy. "It wasn't luck. It was a great deal of time, effort, and money. The balance of power will shift to our side now. It's inevitable."

"It will go worse for you if the Kyrioi believe in your success," the man predicted. He waved at me. "Take care with that one."

I could feel Dorian's body stiffening through his arm. "Etienne, you know that we have ethical disagreements about how that should be accomplished."

"To humanity's cost," Etienne said. It sounded like a rehearsal of a very old argument.

"Might I introduce my cognate?" Dorian said then, pointedly.

Etienne smiled at me then, a dazzling, toothy smile that I recognized had the force of all his persuasion over

8

it. But it washed over me and I felt nothing.

Reluctantly, I extended my hand, and he took it, his grasp cool and dry.

"So pleased to meet you," he said.

I pulled my hand back as quickly as I dared. Dorian's friend or not, the man disturbed me.

"Is that...?" I ventured, my eyes straying to the dreamy-looking woman who floated behind him. I had never met another cognate before, but what else could she be?

She had the false, flawless youth of the agnates but none of the dark power. She cocked her head to the side, and I noticed a red, heart-shaped mark on her neck. Etienne had a matching one just above his collar. Bond marks, like the teardrop-shaped ones that Dorian and I bore on our wrists.

"My own cognate," Etienne said. "Isabella d'Erte."

"Welcome, Isabella," I said, hoping that the expression I wore looked more like a smile than it felt.

The woman just stared at me for a moment, no reaction or recognition in her face, and then her gaze turned back to roaming aimlessly around the room.

"Isabella does not speak English," Dorian said.

"Oh?" I asked.

"She's from Venice," he said briefly.

"She's Italian?" I probed, sensing his reticence. Her reaction had not seemed like that of someone who simply didn't understand the language. It had seemed...empty.

"Byzantine, actually. So her mother tongue is something between vulgar Latin and modern Italian."

Etienne snorted. "Quit coddling the child, Dorian. You're such a hypocrite. If you really wanted your Cora to understand, you would tell her that Isabella no longer speaks at all."

He gave us both a sketch of a bow and strolled off, the woman bobbing mindlessly in his wake.

My stomach clenched. *Run.* I wished I could want to run.

"Dorian...." I said, staring after her in fixated horror. *Isabella no longer speaks at all*—but once, she had. Once, she had been a woman like any other. But then Etienne, through the power of the bond, had changed her into the mindless doll she was now, a woman's body with an empty mind.

"I'm sorry you saw that," he said with soft intensity, putting his free hand over mine. "As I said, we're not all the same."

They weren't the same, but Dorian had already changed me with his very presence, my desires tied to his, and he'd also changed me deliberately, when the stakes were high enough.

What would it take for him to turn me into an Isabella—maybe not today or this year or this decade, but a century from now, half a millennium? To live forever in a twilight existence....

Clarissa materialized in front of us. Her auburn hair was swept up into an elegant chignon, her body clasped in a canary yellow sheath that was slit up to her thigh and widened to puddle in a train behind her.

"Enjoying your party?" she said, clasping our hands in turn, her smile edged and her eyes bright.

She was feeding off the tension in the room. She could sense the danger, too—and unlike me, she loved it.

It was a measure of my state of mind that I found Clarissa's presence almost reassuring. She, at least, was something like a friend.

"I think I'll survive," I replied.

She let out a musical peal of laughter. "You're just *infuriating* them. It's fabulous!" she crowed, and just as quickly as she'd appeared, she ducked back into the crowd and was gone.

Reassuring. Right.

A man in a stiff silk robe popped in front of us before I could say anything, bowing with exaggerated courtesy over my hand.

"Ah, the famous new cognate," he said, every word edged. "What a pretty story you spin about her, Thorne."

"It's no story, and you know it, Timur," Dorian countered.

"Perhaps. You take too many gambles. Throw the dice once too often, and they'll come up snake eyes, and then where will you and your precious Adelphoi be?" With another contemptuous bow, he faded back into the crowd.

I was still reeling when an agnatic woman approached wearing three dead parrots arranged in a macabre tableau on her head. I stared at the budgies as she talked to Dorian, unable to focus on her words, not even to process whether there was bile behind her smile before she left.

"Dorian! And Cora!" A woman came up on the arm of a bored-looking man, her wild blond curls scarcely confined by a silk band.

I blinked because even though it was the woman who spoke, it was the man who had the air of an agnate about him. He wore an expression of bored indulgence.

"Good evening, Dorian," he said.

"Jean, Hattie," Dorian returned. "Allow me to present to you my cognate, Cora Shaw."

I could feel a slight change in his body through my hand on his arm—the tiniest relaxation, and only then did I realize how tense he'd been before.

"A pleasure," Jean intoned, pressing my hand briefly.

"It's excellent to see you up and about," the cognate said briskly as she squeezed my hand in turn. "I wanted to call on you before, but Dorian banished me to the labs as soon as you were awake."

There was something familiar about her, the pretty round face and the mass of curls....

"You were there," I blurted. "When I—I changed. You were there, and you took me away."

Hattie's smile broadened, and her agnate patted her arm with the kind of affection one would show to an excited pet. "You remembered," she said. "I hope Perry Connor didn't frighten you too much."

I shook my head. There had been too much pain for there to be any room for fear.

"Well, enjoy your introduction." She gazed adoringly up into Jean's face. "I certainly loved mine."

"I expect cocktails and baccarat at your New Year's

party," Jean said to Dorian over her head. "You know what I think about parties with neither gambling nor mixed drinks." He frowned at a tray of champagne as a waiter passed by.

"I'm sure that can be arranged," Dorian said.

They turned and left, the parade of greetings continued, each accompanied by varying degrees of enthusiasm or hostility. At times, I couldn't even tell whether their congratulations were meant with sarcasm or sincerity.

Nearly a quarter of the agnates had a cognate in tow. Some of these had the vacant look of Isabella. Others were silent but looked on with intelligent eyes. A few—a very few—spoke to one or both of us, but they all seemed uniformly, almost disturbingly content. I couldn't help but wonder how old they all were—and whether that contentment came of themselves or was a happiness imposed by their agnates.

It was like a bizarre kind of slideshow, a presentation of all my possible futures. My head swam, my stomach roiling. My hand on Dorian's arm began to cramp with the force that I was clinging to him, and my other hand shook when I extended it to be briefly pressed by yet another dazzling agnate. The night had hardly begun, but all I could do was to look forward desperately to the end.

But even when it did, I would be no less trapped, because I feared the futures themselves, not just the presentations of them, because one of them would be mine....

Servants circulated with trays of champagne and

hors d'oeuvres. I took a flute of wine and drank it too quickly, snatching up a second when a waiter came near again and downing it just as fast. Under the sound of the orchestra, the drone of hundreds of conversations echoed through the room.

As Dorian exchanged earnest observations with an older agnatic woman, two children came tumbling up the carpet between the adults, a serious-looking boy with a much younger girl. They stopped short as they realized that I stood in their way.

I stared, my attention pulled from Dorian's conversation. I hadn't noticed any children in the crowd before, the press of adult bodies too great to see smaller ones between them. Somehow, their presence made the gathering more real—and yet more fantastically bizarre.

Both children were astonishingly beautiful. The boy noticed my attention and smirked ingratiatingly under a shock of brown hair, his smile perfectly tuned with complete self-awareness as to its effect. He had his own tail suit, down to the white tie and the wingtip shoes, and he already carried traces of the shadowy authority of the adults and turned its full force on me.

The little girl's velvet skirt stood out like a perfect bell around her, so stiff with petticoats that it rustled with every motion. Her black hair hung in perfect ringlets under a bright purple tiara. Staring at me suspiciously, she rattled the dozen or so plastic beaded necklaces that she wore around her neck, but even that childlike motion was peculiarly, inappropriately elegant.

"We're going to climb that statue," she announced, her tone edged with the contemptuous certainty that I would not dare to cross her.

"Come on," the boy muttered to her, keeping the smile plastered on his face as he stared me down. "She's not human. Let's go around."

"I want to climb up at the *end* of the carpet," the girl said, digging in her heels as he tugged at her hand, little tendrils of will, sensed but not seen, emanating from her. But the older boy overpowered her and dragged her back into the crowd.

Children. Vampire children. The too-perfect facsimiles of humanity in the adult agnates were disconcerting enough, but the children seemed almost like actors, poured into small bodies and playing a role, skillfully hitting all the right notes with the jaded eye of a master manipulator. I was immune, but any true human not under another agnate's thrall would have had her mind turned into mush by one look at those pretty faces.

I shuddered.

"Dorian, darling!"

My attention was jolted to an agnatic woman who came sailing up to us, her dark hair clasped in golden bands. Her goddess-style dress was all white draperies and crisscrossed gold cords that served to emphasize her breasts and the swelling of her pregnant belly.

She was flanked by two muscular, bare-chested men—both non-agnates, I realized—an absurdity even among the varied attire of the other guests. As she advanced, other agnates muttered or stared, and she preened under their disapproval. The men each had an oval mark over their right hip. Both cognates, then? The woman must have a matching mark, invisible beneath her dress.

"I am so glad you finally found someone. Two hundred years of abstinence cannot be healthy." She smiled toothily, thrusting her hand at him.

Dorian bowed over it, wearing a chilly smile. "As delightful as always, Veronica."

"You're such a clever boy," she said. "Now all you need is a second little plaything."

She patted the nearest man proprietarily on the shoulder with one long-nailed hand. With a chuckle, he caught her hand and kissed it, and her expression turned blatantly carnal.

"One is fun, but two are better," she purred.

"You can stop terrorizing my cognate now," Dorian said through his teeth, his smile unwavering. "It isn't gracious to bully your hostess."

"Why, heavens forfend!" She put her hand to her heart and took a deep breath as she turned to me, not coincidentally drawing attention to her generous breasts. "Oh, my dear, are you still such a prude? Don't worry. It never lasts long."

I jerked back automatically as she reached out to touch my shoulder.

She laughed again and cradled her belly. "And who knows? Soon enough, you'll have little ones of your own to think about."

With that, she sashayed off, the men sauntering in her wake.

"Are they really both—" I whispered.

"Yes," he said shortly. "But it's considered very

poor form."

I reached for another flute of champagne as a waiter passed by, but no sooner had I grasped it than Dorian plucked it from my fingers and placed it back on the tray, then took my free hand in his for a brief squeeze.

"You've had quite enough, Cora," he said. "You're doing fine. You don't need that."

His reassurance wrapped around me with almost a physical force, warm and muffling, and I sensed a distant twinge of panic that I could not properly feel.

My head was spinning with all the people and the champagne by the time the orchestra stopped and a bell rang deep in the recesses of the house. The sea of guests began to flow, slowly but steadily, toward the stairs, the buzz of conversation continuing unabated.

Dorian stepped along with them, and I bobbed at his side, anchored to his strength.

"Is it over?" I asked, not quite daring to hope that it was.

"Only the introductions." Dorian looked down at me, studying me closely for the first time since he had stepped down from the top of the stairs. The hard light of victory faded slightly from his eyes, replaced with a hint of pity.

I didn't want his pity. I wanted to escape.

"This is horrible," I said, putting all the force of my feeling in those words. "I want it to be done."

Except it wouldn't ever be done, not really. This was my life with Dorian, in one form or another, forever.

His arm tightened infinitesimally against mine. "I know. I'm sorry. Only dinner and dancing are left. That will likely last until dawn, but we will not be obligated to stay that long."

As we reached the grand staircase and headed down toward the ballroom, I looked at all the beautiful, ageless faces around us and realized that except for the children, I could very well be the youngest person in the room by a hundred years.

"Dancing," I said. "I don't think I can do the kind of dancing that you're talking about."

"But I can," he said. "Have no fear, Cora. You will only be expected to watch the grand march with me and take the first dance, and then you can sit in a quiet corner near the buffet until it is over."

And then I could be put back on the shelf with the other playthings. I knew he had meant to be comforting, but it was anything but. My stomach turned. My place in his world as his cognate seemed to tighten around my throat like a noose. I'd had a future planned, before I'd gotten sick. But the future I wanted and the future demanded of me as Dorian's cognate couldn't both survive.

I braced myself to enter the ballroom.

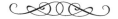

CHAPTER TWO

The back of my neck prickled as we reached the lower level, the memory of the proving that had been held there two nights before bright in my mind. But the tables that had been set up to test Dorian's staff for loyalty were gone now. Every light in the room now shone, even the candelabra on the mirrored walls, and great, thick garlands of roses and lilies hung from them, perfuming the air.

Love and death. How absurdly appropriate.

Another orchestra occupied a raised dais at the far end of the room, now sitting at rest as the agnates and their cognates poured in around us, gathering at the vestibule in front of the dance floor. Four different buffets were set behind the columns that ringed the room, servers standing to attention behind the tables, with golden chairs against the walls in between.

Dorian ignored his guests even as they made way for us, moving aside as we stepped from the marble entry onto the parquet of the ballroom proper.

On cue, the orchestra struck up a stately march. My death grip on Dorian's arm grew even tighter.

"What do I do?" I whispered urgently.

His smile did nothing to put me at ease even as my heart did a little hiccup in my chest. "You walk with me to the viewing platform."

He led the way down the length of the room to a small, elevated stage just below the orchestra's dais. Out of the corner of my eye, I caught movement, but I didn't dare look aside as Dorian stepped up onto the platform. I stumbled after and turned with him to face the assembly.

The guests had paired up down to the smallest of the children and were executing an elaborate choreography in intricate, shifting geometries across the floor, as if there were some giant puppeteer pulling strings above. Every movement was exactly synchronized and so beautiful in its studied grace that it almost hurt to watch.

I was struck with the thought of how deadly those lovely creatures were, the danger in every perfect turn and nod, and I felt like a small, furry animal, mesmerized by the swaying of a snake.

The music swelled and came to a clashing finale just as the entire company turned to face us and bowed.

"And now it is our turn," Dorian murmured. He returned the bow, his gesture low, sweeping, almost exaggerated. Caught off guard, I ducked my head and made a wobbly curtsey at his side.

He straightened and stepped down onto the floor as the assembly faded back. I was pulled along on his arm toward the center of the floor.

"The first dance," I said, a tremor of panic rising in my voice.

"Indeed," he said.

The orchestra began to play a slow, swinging jazz. Not quite what I had expected, but I didn't know what to do with it one bit more than if it had been a waltz. Around us, the couples scattered outward and began to dance around the floor. Even as they whirled past us, I could sense their eyes on us, watching, judging.

Now what?

Dorian shifted the arm I was still holding so that he cupped my shoulder blade, loosening my grip gently and transferring my hand to his shoulder.

"Foxtrot," he said. "My request. It's simplicity itself to follow."

He took my other hand in his free one and raised it, pulling me against him from chest to hip. I closed my eyes at the contact, clinging to the sensation of the hard length of his body against mine—despite everything. The intimacy of it shot through me, bringing a flush of heat to my cheeks and a welcoming blossom of heat deep in my center.

He was the cause of the chaos in my world—and the only still point in it.

Dorian shifted his weight to one foot, pulling me with him, and my eyes flew open again.

"Just feel what I do, Cora," he said, and he stepped out.

I panicked, clenching his arm and stumbling.

"I don't think I can do this," I hissed.

He ducked his head to my ear and murmured, "Don't be afraid. I have you."

The words carried the force of all his persuasion with them, and my anxiety evaporated. I stepped easily with him, his body guiding my own as effortlessly as breathing.

I had been changed again. Panic welled up inside me, churning in my guts, sending my heart lurching sideways. He held me pinned in his arms.

"Don't," I whispered. "Please, don't."

A small frown marred his perfect forehead. "I was trying to help."

"I know," I said as we weaved between other swaying couples. "But stop doing it. I want to be myself. If I'm afraid, then I want to deal with it. I don't want to have it all wiped away for me. That's only one step away from turning me into—into an Isabella."

His arms tightened around me. "I would never do that."

The promise, however treacherous it might be, gave me an infinitesimal reassurance, and the frantic drumming of my heart slowed fractionally. Somehow, my feet never tangled in his, and we never collided with any of the other dancers. The song ended, and he took me on his arm again and led me under the colonnade that encircled the room, heading toward the nearest buffet.

"I have duties as the host to attend to," he said. "But you can have some peace. Nothing will happen to you here."

"How much longer will it be?" I asked. My hand ached from clinging to him.

"Two hours, maybe three. I must make a few rounds of the room—speak to the right people, dance with the right people." He looked down at me, his expression graver than his light words. "I will come for you when I can."

I didn't want to be left alone in a roomful of vampires, even though the irony of clinging to Dorian for defense left a bitter taste in my mouth. Right now, he might very well be more dangerous to me than any of the other agnates.

But I said, "Okay. I'll be here. But if anyone else asks me to dance, I'm refusing."

A ghost of a smile flickered across his face. "Just tell them you're tired. A cognate's prerogative."

A boyish-looking agnate with an unruly mop of yellow hair came up to us. I tried to retrieve his name from the long list of introductions but failed.

"Here I am, Dorian, as promised," he said. Behind him were two uniformed servants.

Dorian shook his hand warmly. "Cora, you remember Tiberius. He'll chase any unwanted attention away." He nodded to the staff. "And if you need anything, send one of them to get me."

"I will," I said. There didn't seem to be anything else to say.

"As soon as we can politely leave, I will come for

you," Dorian promised, and I detected something in his eyes.

Was it reluctance? Or regret?

Tonight was the celebration of the triumph of his work—work that would have taken a human's entire career. It was an event that starkly marked his victory and portended the failure of his enemies. And he was willing to cut that short. For me. Because I was sick and frightened and miserable, he was willing to bow out of his own victory fête.

But I was only here in the first place because he had forced me to attend. How big was the concession, really, when I was giving my life? And how desperate was I, to give him as much credit as I could?

He cupped my cheek briefly, flashed a smile that was edged with possessiveness and a hard triumph, and then he turned away and disappeared into the crowd.

I stood rooted at the edge of the dance floor, hugging myself, feeling more alone in the magnificent crowd than I had all those nights I'd cried myself to sleep in my bedroom after my Gramma died.

Etienne whirled by, Isabella in his arms. Her expression was ecstatic—his was fierce and adoring. I shuddered. How could he look at the mindless doll-woman like that?

"Would you care for some dinner?" Tiberius asked, dragging my attention away from the floor.

The smell of food from the buffet hit me at his words, and I realized that I was hungry. My oversized lunch seemed a very long time ago. I wondered if there was some kind of *Gone with the Wind*-like expectation that ladies would eat delicately. I decided I didn't care.

"Absolutely," I said.

Tiberius held out his arm, radiating charm, and hesitantly, I took it. No reaction went through me at his touch; it appeared that I truly was immune to other agnates. Everyone except Dorian. I let out a breath I hadn't realized I was holding.

"Just sit here," he said, escorting me to one of the armless side chairs against the wall a short distance from the buffet. "I shall bring you a plate."

"How will you know what I like?" I challenged.

His grin was infectious. "I'll get you a little of everything."

There wasn't much to say to that. I sat, the staff members taking positions a short distance away, and Tiberius went off to the far end of the table where the buffet plates were stacked.

My attention was captured by a woman at the buffet whose unkempt hair was haphazardly scraped into a twist. Her ball gown was faded and bedraggled, and she moved with small, jerky motions, muttering continually to herself as she loaded her plate. She was filthy, and my nose burned with her smell as she reached the near end of the table, but her skin shared the peculiarly flawless quality of all the guests, and she had the cast of an agnate about her. Her eyes, when they briefly met mine, were unfocused and confused.

Abruptly, she dropped the fork that she was holding and scuttled away, looking around wildly and clutching her plate with both hands. I shrank back as she passed my chair, so preoccupied that I didn't notice the guest next to me until she spoke.

"Lucky me. I get to sit next to the newest cognate."

CHAPTER THREE

I jumped slightly at the voice so near my ear. A woman had taken the chair next to me, a person I didn't remember being introduced to. Human, I decided—or rather, cognate. She had heavy blonde hair piled on top of her head with tendrils artfully escaping to frame her face. There was something peculiar about her, something unsettling, but I couldn't decide what it was.

"Good evening," I said neutrally, casting a glance at Tiberius.

"I remember my own conversion like it was yesterday," the woman continued. "*God*, I was so naïve! Fifty years old, and yet I knew nothing."

"You don't look fifty," I ventured. In fact, like all the cognates I'd met, she had the same slightly false, plasticky look of youth as the agnates.

She let out a crow of laughter. "No one does unless they want to, sweetie. We look as old as we wish. Eventually, at least. It took thirty years for me to grow young enough for my tastes." She gave a negligent shrug. "Or my master's tastes. I can't remember which."

"So, what, I could be whatever age I wished?" I asked. "Eighty? Or even eight?"

"You can *look* whatever age, within limits," she said. "I believe the youngest cognate I ever met appeared to be approximately fourteen—really, you can't reverse adolescence entirely. The oldest...." She nodded to the floor. "Sixty seems to be as old as most people can manage. A well-preserved, handsome sixty, of course. Wrinkles are hard to maintain, though, so most of them are just showing off for a while. When they get tired of all the effort, they'll go younger again, too. Maybe keep some silver streaks in their hair to look distinguished."

"Oh," I said, not really sure what the proper response was.

The woman rubbed me the wrong way. I didn't have any justification for my reaction, but it remained. I considered manufacturing some excuse to move away, this was still my first chance to speak to any cognate alone. And anyhow, Tiberius was still loading my buffet plate, and I didn't want to lose him in the crush.

"But however you *look*, you will actually *be* whatever age you really are," the woman continued. "Which is now—ageless! Of course, I wasn't this gorgeous, either, back then," she added in a conspiratorial tone, her motion taking in her elegant face and curvaceous body.

"None of us were, but if you bring it up, half the cognates will deny they ever looked any other way."

Which meant that I, too, would change over time. I freely admitted that I found the beauty of all the agnates and cognates intimidating. And there were certainly parts of myself that I didn't much care for, like my nose. But the thought that even my features would inevitably change over time, reshaping like putty, filled me with a slow horror.

"So how did he find you?" The cognate dropped her voice and leaned toward me. "Mr. Thorne claims that his new screening test identified you as a prime candidate. Personally, I think he lost control and went on a bar-raiding rampage but won't admit it."

"I passed a blood test," I said, trying not to bristle in Dorian's defense. "He gave me an opportunity, and after a lot of thought, I took it."

"Knowing the odds?" The woman was openly skeptical.

"I was sort of dying of cancer at the time," I said stiffly. "It was my only shot."

"How very mercenary," she said in a scandalized tone. She took a long drink of her wine. "My story was much more romantic. He was the captain of an Australian prison ship. He had been calling women prisoners in to his cabin, one every night, since the second week of the voyage, and they never came out again. I was so terrified when the boatswain led me in that I pissed myself." She laughed again, as if the story were hysterically funny.

I edged away from her, trying to keep my face

blank.

She continued obliviously. "But then he turned those eyes on me, and I was his. Even if I'd been another body to be heaved over the side in the dead of night, it would have been worth it, just for that time again." Her expression was dreamy. "Every time he marks me, it's just like the first time."

She bent to adjust the ankle strap on her shoe, and the recessed light directly above us shone down on her bare back, revealing a butterfly-shaped red spot just above her waist.

But there was something else, too—a silvery pattern of lines against the snowy expanse of skin. They formed an intricate tracery, brighter lines over fading ones, the layers running together.

As she straightened, I realized that these marks were all over her body, not just her back. Her arms, her throat—even her face bore a few of them.

I had seen something like that before. I tried to think of where. My hand strayed to my neck, and suddenly, I remembered—the healing marks of Dorian's first bite.

My stomach flipped over. It had taken a week for mine to fade away entirely. I tried to imagine the amount of damage that the woman must have sustained to leave so many layers of evidence on her skin. My mind rebelled. I jerked back, and she looked up at my movement, following my gaze to her skin.

"Ah, my love bites," she said, smiling with a languorous sensuality. "Don't you like them?"

"No," I said, standing up so hurriedly that I almost

stumbled.

She gave a girlish giggle, raising her wineglass in a half-salute. "Oh, but you will." She threw back the wine, then wrapped her hand around the bell of the glass and squeezed.

It shattered with a sharp sound, the broken shards slicing into her flesh as she tightened her fingers into a fist around it. Rivulets of blood streamed over her hand, dripping onto the floor.

"Damn," I breathed, backing away.

She smiled up at me and then opened her hand, the piece of glass falling free as her skin closed up again, pushing them out. Her expression was almost ecstatic.

"Oh, Cora," she said. "You don't know what you have to look forward to."

Her words went straight through me, and my guts knotted, hard. It was all too much—the music, the crowd, the awful woman in front of me. Tiberius was headed toward me, carrying an overloaded plate, and his approach was enough to kick my fight-or-flight impulse into overdrive.

Whatever compulsion Dorian had placed on me to stay had faded now. I'd fulfilled my obligations, standing at his side, forcing a smile at his friends. I was done. All I wanted now was to escape—to go back to my campus apartment, hide under my comforter, and pretend that none of this had ever happened. I just wanted my old life back, with my friends and my future and all the hopes and dreams the cancer had taken away from me.

I turned away and fled, charging blindly between agnates and cognates alike.

"Cora!" Tiberius' concerned voice rang out over the conversations.

"Madam. Wait!" I heard the outcry from the other servants behind me, but I ignored them all and pushed onward, bolting for the stairs.

I ducked between two startled agnates, and there it was—the staircase leading up to freedom. Almost woozy with relief, I ran forward—

Only to be caught up short by a hand on my arm.

CHAPTER FOUR

"**H**o ho! It wouldn't be much of a party without the guest of honor."

I spun around.

A male agnate held me, his expression at once avuncular and amused under his carefully tousled light brown hair.

"Let me go," I said tightly.

He dropped my arm immediately, holding up his hand palm-out in a sign of surrender. I got ready to flee again, but his smile was so disarming that I hesitated even as I felt the wave of his persuasion wash over me and leave me untouched.

"Dorian can be a bit of a boor," he said. "Such a stickler for propriety. He could have waited a week or two before throwing you into all this, to let you get your bearings. But he just had to go by the rules and introduce you within ten days of your conversion."

It was the first I'd heard of any such rule. As far as I knew, the date had been picked to put an end to people trying to kill me.

"Who are you?" I asked bluntly. I was pretty sure he'd not joined the line of congratulations earlier, and his jocular familiarity now made me wonder why.

He held out his hand. "Cosimo Laurentis."

I took it suspiciously, but he gave it a perfectly polite shake.

"Cora Shaw," I said.

"Cora Shaw, Cora Thorne, it all depends on your preference now," he said. "And of course Dorian's. But that goes without saying, *cara.* Come back to the party. Dorian will be so disappointed if you leave."

"I don't care," I said, backing toward the stairs.

"But you will," he pointed out with a smile. "As soon as Dorian finds you."

I stopped. I couldn't deny the truth of that. His caring would make me care. And that horrified me almost as much as the marks on that woman's skin.

"Come now, *bella,"* he cajoled. "I know it's stressful, with all the worst members of agnatic society here. But chin up, and all that. It's only one night."

"The worst?" I repeated, still feeling slightly nauseated. "Do you include yourself in that description?"

Cosimo chuckled. "Oh, most definitely."

He offered me his arm. Better the devil you know, the old phrase went. Except I didn't know Dorian's world. Not yet. If I was being dragged into it, I needed to—even though that was most definitely not what the saying meant.

34

I hooked my arm around his, and he led me back through the crowd at the edge of the dance floor to the shelter behind the colonnade. "There you go, *cara*. I'll get you some food and champagne."

I nodded, taking the nearest seat, and Cosimo disappeared into the crowd.

The crowd was thinner this far from the buffet. I saw no other cognates, but a clutch of agnates laughed uproariously a short distance away, having commandeered several bottles of wine and pulled some of the chairs into a circle at the edge of the dance floor. Several were slumped over, blinking slowly, and as I watched, one produced a syringe and casually filled it, tapping her vein several times before plunging it in.

That couldn't possibly be legal. I tried to make myself invisible against the wall, but they showed no interest in anything that happened outside their group.

With a flourish, a male produced a baggie with a line of white pills in the bottom. He poured the contents into his hand, and he tossed them up in the air to whoops and hollers of delight. As the agnates scrambled to catch them, two men collided hard.

What happened next was almost too fast to see. One moment, they were crashing drunkenly into each other—the next, the large one had lifted the smaller one by the neck and flung him a good twenty feet onto the ballroom floor.

The dancers dodged with inhuman nimbleness, all except a consort who ended up being clipped by the man's flailing leg, but even he was caught before he hit the ground and lifted out of the way of further harm.

The orchestra broke off, and the thrown agnate lay still on the ground. A sudden silence spread like a shockwave through the room.

Was he dead? I stood up, not knowing what to do. Should I call 911? Could paramedics even help a vampire?

But then the man lurched to his feet, shaking his head, and he gave a roar and rushed back toward his attacker with the same inhuman speed.

The room seemed to implode as other vampires rushed toward the two brawlers. In an instant, both the assailant and the victim were pinned under the weight of a dozen bodies, then dragged to their feet and unceremoniously hustled up the stairs.

Dorian appeared at my side, his eyes blazing. "What are you doing here?" he demanded.

"I was getting away from a horrible woman—"

He took my arm, sweeping me along with him. "Did I not tell you that all society would be coming tonight? Most of these people are not my friends."

"I'm sorry," I blurted, frightened by his fury.

He stopped. We were now at the other end of the ballroom from where the fight had broken out. "No, Cora. I am sorry. I was trying not to scare you, and I put you in danger."

"I thought you said I was safe now," I said weakly. "Safe from any agnate here."

"Against deliberate attempts to harm you. That group, though, in their current state...." He shook his head.

"Who were those people? Those agnates?" I corrected.

"Agnates are people, too," he said. "And they were one of the more unsavory elements of society. You have drug addicts and daredevils—we have rushers, who are all that and more." He squeezed my shoulder gently. "I will answer all your questions later. Introductions have conventions that are broken only at our peril, but it does you a great disservice. Please, Cora, stay here, with the servants and Tiberius. He will chase away anyone who is bothering you. Just give him the chance. I have obligations that I must fulfill, but I'll come for you as soon as I can."

I blinked at him as I realized that despite the intensity in his voice, there was no force of compulsion behind it. He wasn't making me stay—he truly was asking. Had my plea on the dance floor really meant something to him, then?

"I just want to leave now," I said. "I've seen enough. Heard enough. I just want to go."

His expression softened. "That would not be a good idea. Be brave, Cora. I promise you that our cause is worth fighting for."

He kissed me gently, chastely on the lips and left me with my nerves jangled, standing next to the buffet table, Tiberius at my elbow and a circle of servants around me.

Alone again, though in the crowd. Trapped again.

Numbly, I ate the dinner that Tiberius had brought, drinking far too much from the wineglass I put at my feet. The guests paraded through the buffet near me, and Clarissa joined me briefly until my short answers and long silences sent her restlessly into the ballroom again.

The two children I'd seen earlier reappeared, hovering near the buffet until one of the servers looked away. Seizing the opportunity, they swiped an entire plate of finger-cakes and ducked under the edge of the heavy table skirt with their plunder. There was no sign of them except the occasional giggle until a woman in a plain black dress suddenly appeared. I straightened slightly as I realized that, like the servers, she was fully human.

With unerring direction, she went straight to the table and jerked up the edge of the skirt.

"There you two scamps are!" she exclaimed in a crisp British accent. "Come out this moment."

"Go away." The boy's voice was clear and firm, and in it, I heard every ounce of influence that he could muster.

The woman swayed for a moment, and then an expression of indignation crossed her face. "You little monster! You tried to enthrall me. I don't know where you got my blood, but I'm telling your mother, and you'll be on restriction for a month."

"I told you it wouldn't work." The little girl's whisper carried easily from under the table.

"Shut up, Anna," the boy snapped. He climbed out, looking shamedfaced. "I'm sorry, Miss Goring," he said, every word infused with a sincerity I was certain he didn't feel.

"Oh, you will be," the woman said, but already the conviction in her voice was slipping—the thrall had some effect, after all. She stooped to peer into the shadows of the table. "Your governess is looking for you, too. You'd best get out, or your father will hear of it."

The words were meant to be tart, I was sure, but a note of indulgence had crept in.

"Yes, Miss Goring," said the girl resentfully. She clambered out, too, all smeared with chocolate frosting, and Miss Goring walked off with them on either side.

As I watched, she petted the boy's head affectionately, then absently hugged the sticky girl against her hip. The last traces of irritation faded from her face to be replaced with a soft smile. I caught a glimpse of the boy smirking at the girl around the woman's skirt before they were swallowed in the crowd.

I pushed the plate onto the chair next to mine, no longer hungry. Those children were budding sociopaths, with their slippery, reflexive manipulations that eroded the wills of every human they came into contact with.

Yet they were the future that Dorian had planned for me.

I emptied my wineglass quickly, setting it down again a little too hard. The lights, the music, the glittering crowd—it all ran together then. I hugged myself as the swirling skirts turned into a whirling muddle of color, the strains of the orchestra bleeding into the murmured conversations.

And over and over, the same thoughts circled in my mind: There had to be a way out. Whatever the cost, there had to be a way out.

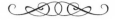

Chapter Five

I opened my eyes, and for a disorienting moment, I didn't know where I was. I blinked at the silhouettes of furniture, encircled by the shadowy bookcases around the perimeter of the room.

Dorian's study, I thought sluggishly, though it was now shrouded in darkness, the only light coming from a fire burning in the grate. And I was lying on the sofa, still dressed in the green ball gown with a heavy blanket laid over me.

"I was beginning to wonder if you were asleep for the night." Dorian lounged in a club chair near the fire, his feet up on an ottoman and a brandy in his hand. His tailcoat and vest were tossed over the arm of the chair, his white tie dangling loose from either side of his open collar.

I had the vague memory of a firm chest against my body, strong arms lifting me up, and the words in my ear: "Hush, now."

"Is the party over?" I asked. The dread I had felt was still there, deep in my gut, but it was dampened now by the drug of Dorian's presence. The firelight played over the planes of his face, gilding the prominence of his cheekbone and the line of his nose and jaw.

"More or less. Some of the guests will be here until they are politely ejected at dawn," Dorian said, regarding me steadily over the rim of his glass.

"You left them? Even though I was asleep?"

His shrug was negligent. "Our duties are over now. My allies can make sure that the guests who remain do not get into too much trouble. I thought you'd like to leave, awake or not. And I also thought you might have a few questions for me."

"A few," I echoed. That didn't even begin to cover it.

A shadow of a smile passed across his face. "Where would you like to start?"

"Etienne and Isabella," I said immediately, straightening up and pushing the blanket off. "How could you be friends with a man who would do something like that to his—his cognate?" I stumbled a little over the word.

Dorian sighed, looking suddenly ancient and remote. "Not all agnates agree with my research. Etienne sees the value in it. His endorsement carries a great influence among many. He is a cornerstone of the Adelphoi."

"Adelphoi. What is that?" I asked.

"The Adelphoi are my allies," he said. "Versus the Kyrioi, who believe that agnates are properly the lords of humans. The history of our people goes back long before our memories hold out. But we believe that we are the creation of the union of men and angels—fallen angels, who wished to create a beautiful, corrupt race to have dominion over the race of men."

"We believe," I repeated. "Do you believe it, too?"

His mouth twisted slightly, an emotion passing over it so quickly that I couldn't identify it before it was gone. "It isn't something that you human-born can understand. Your kind are born and die in the space of only a few years, and everything is changed or forgotten in a few repetitions."

He turned the brandy glass so that the firelight glinted off the cut facets of the crystal. "Our traditions are stronger. Eighty of your generations would have been born in the time it takes one agnate's memory to unravel, and our retellings change less, as the overlapping of our lives into the distant past leads to a greater consistency. Some of the youngest agnates think our origin story just a peculiar myth, but it is something that I and all those of my age have held as a certainty as far back as my mind disappears into the fog of time."

"So you actually believe that you are...demonspawn?" I said. "I mean, that's what fallen angels are supposed to be, right? Demons? That's...that's terrible."

"Why else must we kill to live? We were made for evil," he said heavily. The darkness seemed to knit itself more tightly around him, the pulsing agnatic influence almost tangible.

"Some of us embrace it, believing that we must be true to that nature, as the natural lords of men." His gaze transfixed me. "No human can refuse us, Cora. They all go willingly to their deaths. Humans are masters of the beasts of the field, and those creatures don't even give themselves up. Who is to say that what we do is wrong? And even if it were, is wrongness not defined by those who are opposed to our own creators?"

"But we aren't animals," I protested.

"And we aren't human. It's not my argument, Cora. And it's not my belief, but that of those who oppose what I do."

He took a drink of his brandy, emptying it swiftly, and set the glass on the table next to his chair. "These others, the Kyrioi, believe that to defy our natures is misguided at best and self-destructive at worst. And they were right about the self-destruction, because many of us would not live long enough to find a cognate if we restrained our feedings to what our bodies demanded. Until now."

"Because of your research," I said.

"Because of you," he corrected. "The result of my research. The first of many. The Adelphoi believe that we might have been created for evil, but we still have the chance of redemption, the same chance any man might have. We have to. We can't be damned by our births."

"The rising angel," I said, remembering the statue.

"The rising angel or the falling demon," Dorian

43

agreed. "We must have the power to choose which to be."

"Then how can Etienne be one of you?" I demanded, standing in my restless irritation. "How can he think that brainwashing Isabella will...will redeem him?"

Dorian tipped his head back, looking up at me. Even as he sat with the loose-limbed grace of a cat, he looked no less dangerous. No less compelling.

"To have a consort saves lives. Hundreds, perhaps thousands, depending on how long he or she lives. Etienne believes that human lives matter, and he also believes that many lives matter more than one. And what he's done has kept her safe and subjectively happy for twelve hundred years. She may be the oldest cognate in the world."

Twelve hundred years. For twelve centuries, she had been a husk of a woman, emptied out, a blood donor kept one step above a vegetable. I couldn't even wrap my mind around that length of time, even as my brain kept going through the brutal arithmetic: sixty of my lifetimes, forty of my mother's, twenty of my grandmother's....

Dorian continued mercilessly. "At a minimum, we must feed three times a year for sanity and life. Four a year for functional health. Her survival has spared at least that many. "

My mind shifted thoughts abruptly. And he had lived how long? *Older than empires,* he had said. *Older than memory.* Two thousand years? Three?

How many had he killed?

"And you?" I asked, the question dragged from me by my need to know. "How many lives a year do you—did you—take?"

"Four." The answer was flat.

I rubbed the mark on my wrist. Thousands of lives, then. Many thousands. The man to whom my life was bound had killed more people than Ted Bundy, Charles Manson, or the Son of Sam—or all of them combined. He made Jack the Ripper look like a dilettante. Only a tyrant or a war criminal could match his monstrosity.

And yet I could feel the pull of him from here, his dark beauty like a drug in my veins, calling to me in a way that no man ever had. I had let him do things to me that no one ever had done before, and I'd do it all over again.

Even if I knew every name. Even if I saw every face of those who had come before me.

What kind of monster was he? I scoffed at the question. He, at least, was what he was born to be. The real question was, what kind of monster was I?

"And that's what you want me for," I said. "To give you blood. To give you children. So that your damned Adelphoi win."

"That's part of what I wanted a cognate for. But also...to be whole. Alive." He held out his hand in the firelight, studying it as if it belonged to someone else. "Like waking from a long dream." His eyes snapped back up to my face. "But you—no, that's not all I want *you* for. Though I would feel for any cognate, that does not mean it would be the same feeling, Cora, nor are rational motives identical with emotional realities."

I shook my head, not understanding. "You don't even know me. You don't even care who I am."

"Don't I?" he returned.

"You've never met my friends," I said. "You don't know my hobbies. I don't even think you know my major, or my high school, or my grades, or anything about my family. All you know are a few things that I did."

"The other things, they're minutiae." He made a dismissive gesture with his fingers. "They're details about your life. They don't say anything about who you are or who you will be."

"What does, then?"

"Your actions, of course." His gaze raked across me. "I know you more intimately than you imagine. You're the girl who fights with every fiber of her being for the dreams she made into her reason for hanging on to life, even when tempted with wealth and pleasure beyond her imagination. You're the girl who defeated a djinn and escaped an agnate's mind-slaves. You're the girl who looked at the woman who nearly killed her and forgave, completely and instantly, when she understood that the woman had done nothing with intent. You're the girl who tried to defy her own agnate when she found his terms intolerable to her sensibilities."

"And when I tried to refuse to do that one thing, you just about popped off the top of my skull and rummaged around, like it was nothing," I said, the bitter edges of my words hurting my throat.

"If I hadn't, you would have died." His answer was quiet.

"Died? Because you would have killed me?" I scoffed, circling behind the sofa.

"My enemies would have seen to that. If you hadn't shown up tonight, you would have forfeited the temporary protection the invitations afforded you."

"But what if it was only the Adelphoi's victory that was at risk?" I asked. "Would you have let me walk away then?"

Dorian looked at me, and I knew he could make me believe anything he said. Why did I imagine that he'd give me the truth?

But he surprised me. Because he did.

"No," he said. "I wouldn't let you walk away. We have only two choices, Cora. We can reach for heaven or fall to hell."

I wanted to shake him in frustration. "What does that have to do with me?"

His words were heavy. "If I made the selfish choice, the choice that would please you, at the cost of my ideals, it would be that much easier to go against them the next time. And the next time, the breech may not be something that you would choose."

"If," I said. "What does that even mean, *if*?" It seemed to me like a coward's word, something that could be used to justify anything.

"The next time, perhaps I wouldn't please you. Perhaps I would please my baser instincts instead," he said evenly.

I glared at him. How dared he act like he'd been doing me a favor? "You did please yourself, though. You made me go, and that's what you wanted."

Dorian unfolded from his chair and crossed to where I hovered between the sofa and the door. He stood so close that I could feel his legs against my skirt, and I half raised one hand to touch his chest before I caught myself and dropped it again.

He looked down at me, his eyes hard and bright in the shadows. "No. I didn't want you merely to go. I wanted you to be happy to be there with me. To be happy to be with me always."

Always. I shivered at the finality of the word.

"I took the least evil path that I could see," he continued. "I kept you safe. And I worked for the greater good while requiring as little from you as I could."

"Requiring little? You want me to have your children!"

"It won't be against your will," he said. He reached out and brushed my cheek with the barest touch of his fingers, and a deep, keening need wound through me.

"You'll change my will." The words were a whisper.

He shook his head. "No, Cora. I won't. Ten years—that's half your lifetime now. How can you be so sure what you will want in ten years? Or twenty? Or fifty?"

I could feel in my body the desire to please him, a yearning for his approval. And right and wrong always seemed so slippery when I was with him, everything I thought I knew shifting under my feet. How long would it be until even that final step seemed like a small concession?

And would it be him who caused the change, then?

Or the bond? Or me? Could I ever even know?

"How can I want you?" I didn't realize I had said the words aloud until they reached my own ears. "God, this bond—it's crazy."

"You may look upon what we have in horror, but how do you think we regard your human relationships? Your affections wax and wane." Contempt dripped from every word even as he trailed his hand down my neck and across my shoulder and arm, his touch sending shards of desire through me as he seemed to drink me with his eyes. "You marry for love but also for convenience, from tradition, for stability and companionship, for money, for children, or simply because people expect it of you."

I swayed in the force of his regard, but I couldn't deny what he said.

He continued, "And what you feel on your wedding night and what you feel five years later, ten, twenty, forty—even true love may not last, or it may blossom and fade several times over. We are as constant as the sun. Our hearts are not our own to give, but once they are taken, they do not—they cannot—waver." He reached my hand and took it, clasping it in his own.

Another jolt went straight through my body even as my mind rebelled at his words. He was equating a bond—our bond—with love, but there was nothing that I had seen that night that was anything like the kind of love I believed in. Not even Jean and Hattie, with him acting as if she were a child to be indulged and talked around.

"How can you talk about it like that? A heart—

what can you even know about a heart, other than its blood? That's not love," I protested.

He might believe it was, but being a vampire, how could he even know what love should be?

"You know better than that, Cora. There's more than blood between us. Humans pretend to value unconditional love, but that's not something full humans could ever understand. There are always conditions—lines that cannot be crossed, words that cannot be unsaid." He raised the back of my hand to his lips, and my skin came alive under his touch.

"But with you, no line is too far," I said faintly, through the sensations that he stirred in me. "It never can be. Nothing is too much, even if it destroys me. "

"I would sooner destroy myself," he said, and his next kiss fell on my lips.

I clung to him, my body pressed against his, my parted lips inviting him to take me. But the kiss was too soft, over too soon as he moved lower, along my jaw and down my neck.

Need flared up in the core of my being, pushing up my spine and into my brain. I knew what was going to happen next—I knew it, and I wanted nothing else but him. Even though I refused the names he wanted to put to what we had.

CHAPTER SIX

Flames of desire licked across my skin, following his mouth as it traced the neckline of my dress and swirling into my mind. I struggled against its influence, trying to keep a clear head. Maybe my surrender was inevitable, but I wouldn't give up easily.

"This—this is just lust," I said. "Chemicals. Like an animal in heat."

He straightened, standing over me, and my hands tightened slightly, involuntarily on the fabric of his shirt.

"Your greatest poets would disagree," he said. "Those who are supposed to be able to put words to the human condition with more skill than any."

I shook my head even as one of his hands found the zipper of my dress and pulled it down, sending a shock of anticipation through me. "I don't believe you."

"'Let not the marriage of true minds admit impediments,'" he recited as the stiff fabric of the dress's bodice came away from my body. "'Love is not love which alters when it alteration finds.'"

He tugged at the gown, and it slid over my hips to puddle at my feet. His hands came to rest lightly on my waist, still encased in the heavy foundation garment.

"That's not what those words mean," I protested even as my body inclined toward his involuntarily. He was changing things around, just like he always did.

"Isn't it?" Dorian stepped around, behind me. I stood with the dress billowing around my ankles, caught in the force of his darkness. My body felt stretched, tense, waiting for his next touch.

And then it came, and I gasped as his lips touched the nape of my neck, moving down across the prominence of my spine, smooth and cool against my skin. The heat in my center pooled low, where my legs joined. I leaned into him, closing my eyes, losing the edges of myself in the electric reaction.

He pulled away just far enough to speak, and I felt his breath against my skin.

"'Love is not love which alters when it alteration finds,'" he repeated softly, "'or bends with the remover to remove.'"

I shivered at those words. No, nothing I could do seemed to be able to erase the way I reacted to Dorian, no matter how strongly I willed it. I knew I had to escape the terrible bond that held me—but I was afraid that if someone offered me the chance right then, when I was in his arms, I could do nothing but refuse.

And I was also afraid that I wanted more from him

than what the words *sex* or even *pleasure* could encompass. When he touched me like that, I had a mad urge to immolate myself in him until I was utterly lost, so that I didn't even know who or what I was anymore. And I was afraid that if I did—when I did—he might not put me back together again.

I felt his hands move to the laces of the corset, and I caught my breath as he untied them, anticipating the cool air. But instead, he put a hand between my shoulder blades and pulled.

The pressure against my ribs and waist increased so abruptly that the air was pushed from my lungs. He moved his hand to my hips and pulled again. I felt the open inch at the back of the foundation garment come closed, pressing on me so that I had to take shallow breaths from my chest.

"What are you doing?" I asked as he tied the laces off again.

He chuckled, a dark, rich sound that made my hair rise on the back of my neck. He pulled me back against his body, his mouth exploring the curve of my neck. "You will see," he murmured as his lips skimmed my ear.

Dorian wrapped his arms around my waist, but I could hardly feel them through the pressure of the corset. Then his mouth found my collarbone, followed it, and my body trembled against his as he found its hollow. He kissed his way up the side of my neck to the sensitive place just behind my ear. My skin felt hot and flushed, his lips and tongue sending shivering reactions through me that left my legs loose and shaky.

He turned me in his arms, and my body melded to his, fitting so well that it frightened me. He caught my mouth, a light, brief kiss that left my lips tingling for more. My breath came fast against the stricture of the corset, and I let out a little sound as his mouth came down over mine again. The kiss was firmer but still too brief, a mere press of his lips to mine before it was gone. I ached between my thighs, and the satin lining of the corset rasped against my skin. My arms had wrapped around his body, holding him to me. I wanted him closer, closer still....

He gave a sad, distant half-smile as he looked down at me, and at the sight of it, my heart squeezed in my chest.

"'Love is an ever-fixed mark that looks upon tempests and is never shaken,'" he said, almost to himself. "'It is the star to every wandering bark, whose worth's unknown, although his height be taken.'"

Worth unknown. Again the words meant almost too much. What was the meaning of what I felt? I would have labeled it lust, if I had been forced to give it any name at all, but that didn't begin to cover it. What I wanted wasn't just his body on mine. I wanted to erase those flashes of sadness, to melt his coldness, to fill the ancient emptiness within him with myself.

And a part of me wanted him not to admit that he didn't love me—but to prove that he did.

That discovery froze me in place, struck with a bone-deep terror. I couldn't want him, no matter what, because what he offered me was nothing but a beautiful prison. What he felt about me couldn't possibly matter.

Could it? If I really thought that, why did I keep pushing him, asking him?

I don't care, I told myself fiercely. *I don't. I won't.*

Then Dorian kissed me again, and the shock it sent rippling through me seemed to mock all my resolutions. I could taste him as he dipped shallowly between my lips, and I felt a sudden, half-panicked desperation for more, for everything, and I opened my mouth, begging him in.

But he pulled away, and I gave a tiny, involuntary whimper.

"Well, then," he murmured, and again that chuckle, as dark and rich as his brandy-flavored mouth. This time, when his mouth met mine, it was everything I had been yearning for. He possessed me utterly, stroking my tongue, my mouth, moving with a slow rhythm that rocked my body, tying my brain and my hips and my lips and my center to him. And the strange desperation twisted into a kind of exulting fulfillment. *Yes, this, this and more....*

The ache between my thighs deepened to a throb, and he caught me up against him as my legs gave way. Scooping me up, he carried me to the sofa.

His eyes were haunted as he set me down softly upon the leather. "'Love alters not with Time's brief hours and weeks, but bears it out—even to the edge of doom.'"

Whose doom? His, or mine?

Could it even matter?

He started to pull away, but I clung to his shirt.

"Don't," I said. *Don't leave.*

He treated me to a lopsided smile that hurt my heart. "Have no fear, Cora. I'm not going anywhere."

He loosened my hands from his shirt and slid his away to unclip the white suspenders that held up his highwaisted pants. I sat up and pulled the tail of his shirt out of the waistband of his pants and loosened the bottom stud. I kept my head down as I worked upwards, not wanting to see the shadow of myself reflected in his eyes.

His hands, working down, met mine halfway. He caught my hands in his, and I stilled, my body thrilling at even that small contact.

"Cora," he said, and my eyes were dragged upward. I saw the shadow there, but over it was a hunger that sent my pulse skittering out of control.

"I don't understand what's happened to me," I said weakly.

"It's good, Cora," he said, bending to bring my hand to his lips, just as he had the first time we had been together. I closed my eyes at the silken caress, soft and hard at once. I could feel his breath against the back of my knuckles. "It is the purest thing in my black life."

And the blackest one in mine?

Dorian let go of my hand and knelt next to the sofa. He captured one of my ankles in his hands and slid the shoe from my foot. His thumbs moved against my instep slowly, methodically, releasing tension that I didn't even know I had, working into my heel and the across the ball of my foot. I sank back against the sofa's arm as liquid warmth filled me, all my muscles gone limp.

And something within me let go and surrendered to the moment, whatever it might bring.

I watched with half-lidded eyes as he lifted my foot and bent his head. But it wasn't until I felt his damp mouth against the arch that I realized what he was doing.

Embarrassment flooded me. How could he put his mouth there, on my foot, of all places? I had the urge to snatch my foot away, but then what I was feeling penetrated my brain, and I couldn't move.

It should tickle, I thought dimly. Oh, but it did not. The delicious sensations of his lips and tongue and, yes, teeth were anything but ticklish. He kissed each toe separately, then slipped one into his mouth and suckled it in a way that sent a lance of pleasure straight into my groin.

As I was still gasping in surprise, he slipped off my other shoe and repeated the performance on that foot. I had slipped into a pleasant, achy haze when his mouth moved upward, to the space just behind my ankle.

Dorian skimmed quickly over my calves to linger against the tender skin of my inner knee, first one and then the other. The lassitude I had felt was heating to a more tense anticipation, tightening deep in my belly and making my breath come faster against the unyielding clasp of the corset.

He slid his hands up my legs, nudging them apart. His mouth followed, damp and insistent, against the tender skin of my inner thighs. The closer he got to their juncture, the tighter the tension coiled in my center, and aching so much that I grabbed his wrists to keep from touching myself.

Dorian's mouth reached the edge of my panties, and I inhaled sharply as he kissed it slowly and then ran his tongue under the elastic. There, he was right there, and my body burned with the intensity of what I wanted him to do next. I couldn't even think it, much less put words to it, but a part of my brain started on an endless loop: *Oh please, please, there, please there, please....*

He kissed me softly though the cotton, his hot breath going through it and sending a surge of reaction through my body that left me lightheaded. He hooked his fingers under the band and tugged. The panties slid from under my rear and down my legs. He pulled his hands free from mine and dropped the garment to the side.

Dorian rocked back, and I shook with the withdrawal. But I bit off a noise of protest when I saw his hands at the fly of his pants as he got up. A moment later, he'd toed off his shoes and socks and stripped from the waist down. He stood before me for a moment in nothing but his open shirt, the firelight flickering off the pale, perfect contours of his body, his proud erection darker than the marble purity of his skin.

It still amazed me that such a strange thing had been inside me. And even more astonishing, I had wanted it, panted for it each time, just as I ached for it now.

"Not yet," Dorian said, the smile playing at the corner of his lips for once unshadowed by darker thoughts.

My eyes snapped up to meet his gaze, and I realized

that my hunger had been naked on my face. I bit my lip, and his smile broadened.

"In time, Cora," he said, lowering himself onto the empty half of the sofa. "In time."

He swiftly traced a line up from my knee to the crease of my thigh with his mouth, lips and tongue almost unbearable against my sensitive skin.

And then he was there, at the aching entrance to my body, before I was ready yet also too long after. His kiss was a damp, light, closed-mouth caress that sent me reeling. He kissed me again there, his mouth in my curls, my half-open legs baring my folds to his mouth, and I tilted my hips toward his touch.

Never had I imagined, never, never…. The word seemed to tangle with the light pressure of his mouth and the feelings he sent through me. Never, never, never that it could be like *this*.

My heart beat fast in my ears. I struggled to catch my breath against the tightness of the corset. I could feel his breath on me, and I gripped the corset at my hips, jamming my fingers under the stiff edge, needing something to hold onto for what I knew was coming next.

And it came. The full width of his tongue, pushing between the outer folds at the lowest point of my entrance, moving upward so slowly, too slowly until it stopped to rest against my clitoris. Heat surged through me. I knew that he must feel it, too, feel my swelling against his mouth. I couldn't breathe. I couldn't think. My brain was too full, everything was too full, swollen, aching, needing.

Then he was gone, and I drew a shaky breath, but too soon—already he was back, spreading me with his tongue, moving upward to rest against me again, even more intimately. I whimpered and squirmed into him. His hand slid under me, his thumb skimming slickly over the pad of skin until he reached the bottom edge of my opening.

I took a sharp breath as he pushed in, between my folds, and then he pulled downward, putting pressure against it and sending a jolting reaction up and down the juncture of my thighs. I tightened against him, panting, as the hot tingling reached almost to my tailbone.

Keeping his thumb in place, he began to tease around my entrance with his mouth, planting tiny kisses and nibbles along my folds and—*oh, God*—my clit until I moaned at my fullness.

His only response was that wicked, rich chuckle, the one that sent my heart racing, and I could feel the reverberation of it where his now closed mouth still touched me. And then his tongue was torturing me again, methodically. His touch was frustratingly light, hardly dipping between my folds. I fought the constraint of the corset to try to arch my hips toward him until he took my clit into his mouth and gave it a long suck that tore a cry from me as my shoulders rocked up from the sofa.

His mouth grew harder, more insistent then, pushing deeper. His thumb slid out of me, and I gasped with the sudden relief until he began massaging just below, in time with his mouth, bringing a new tension to my body.

Then he lifted his head, his gaze catching mine as two fingers of his other hand followed the slick path his mouth had made, pushing deep inside as my body made little, shaking spasms around it.

"I've wanted to see you like this from the first moment I saw you," he said as he moved his hand slowly inside me.

It almost hurt to look at him, to let him see everything that he was doing to me, but I couldn't tear my eyes away. His fingers were inside me, sliding and rocking against me—my body sang with them, as if they were touching my soul. The corset was an unbearable pressure. I gasped for air, fighting for it, and it only made the sensations more intense, the sharpness of the pleasure edging into pain.

And then something snapped, and I went over into the heat of it, the wave rippling up through me. He smiled as he saw me go—and then he lowered his head again, his mouth joining his fingers. At that touch sensation surged into my center and through my limbs until even my toes and fingers burned with it.

I gulped for air that would not come, fought against the darkness and the stricture of the corset that now added a new torture, as if it seared my skin even as it conformed my body to it. I heard a voice, a strangled and wordless cry, and I realized it was mine. And he pushed me through it, pushed me deeper into it, his hands and mouth driving me onward until I thought I would be lost forever.

Slowly, slowly the sensation receded. Dorian moved away from my entrance, intolerably swollen now, sliding up the length of my body and catching my neck in one damp hand.

Damp from me, was my dazed realization.

"Taste it," he said. "Taste how good you are."

And his lips met mine, and I tasted the flavor of his mouth mingled with my musky, salty sweetness. The shock of it went through me. It should have disgusted me—the thought of it would have disgusted me any time before. But now it made me whimper into his mouth, wanting more, needing even more.

His hips were already between my legs, the head of his erection against the crease of my thigh. I tried to arch my hips toward him, but the edge of the corset just bit cruelly into my belly.

"What do you want?" Dorian murmured against my mouth. "Tell me, Cora. Say it."

"You." I could say nothing else.

And then he shifted and slid into me, and I tilted into him with all the force the corset would allow, sliding up until our pelvises met. I clenched my teeth against my own whimper as he rocked up so that he pressed his weight up against my clit even as he pushed against my deepest place. My palms and my face were burning, and my breaths had little catching sounds at the end as I forced them from my body.

He thrust into me, the rhythm lost in my heartbeat and the throbbing heat that rose up around me. Around us. Because even Dorian's cool chest warmed against mine as he drove onward, filling me completely, over and over again. It was almost too much, so close to pain, so close to losing myself.

The embrace of the corset was merciless, stealing my breath, stealing my thoughts, keeping me off balance so that when I fell, I went over hard, back into darkness. I clung to Dorian, my nails digging into his skin, and then suddenly his arms went from supporting his weight to holding me against him as if he were afraid that I might be snatched away, and he buried his face in my hair as his whole body shuddered in the grasp of his own climax.

I was still shaking with the aftermath as he slowed, slowed and stopped and lay heavy against me. I lifted my hands to my cheeks and discovered wetness there. My tears.

I had to be free. But how on earth was I ever going to give him up?

CHAPTER SEVEN

Dorian smiled above me and kissed the tears away.

"That bad?" he said, and the tone of smug self-satisfaction betrayed it for the joke that it was.

"That good, and you know it," I said hoarsely. I was too weak, too spent for a better retort than that.

He pulled back, and I ached to feel him go even as I couldn't imagine pressing on. He stood, then bent and lifted me in his arms as if I weighed nothing at all.

"Let's get you dressed, and then I'll take you home," he said. But his arms around me tightened at that last word.

Home, to my apartment at the University of Maryland. To the life that I had there. The idea of separation came as a physical pain.

"But I want to stay," I said. "Please, let me stay with you."

They were stupid words, but I couldn't stop them. They were the wrong words—I shouldn't want to stay. I needed to go, to get away, to escape from the future that was laid out in front of me—even to the edge of doom.

There was a flash of something across his face then, pain or joy or regret, or perhaps all three. He looked like he was going to speak. But instead, he kissed me, slowly and deeply, whether to silence me or himself, I didn't know. And his arms relaxed.

When he pulled back, his face was closed again. "No, you don't, Cora. Perhaps at this instant you feel that you do. But tomorrow, you'll be filled with regret and anger, and you'll wonder whether you wanted to stay at all or if I had merely wanted it for you."

"And do you?" I whispered. I knew what he could do to me—I knew it all too well.

"More than anything right now," he said, and for a second, the shutters drew back from his eyes, and what I saw there made my head feel light. "Which is why you must go. I don't trust myself with you tonight."

He was walking toward a bookcase on the side of the fireplace. He freed a hand and pressed a hidden button, and it swung outward to reveal a spiral stair, a soft light coming on as the concealed door opened.

A secret passageway. Of course he had one.

"Why?" I asked, my heart rising into my throat even as I clung to him. "What are you afraid that you will do?"

"Change you, so that you will never want to leave," he said simply as he mounted the stairs.

"You changed me today," I challenged. He'd changed me, and I knew he would do it again, if the stakes were high enough. "I didn't want to go to your Lesser Introduction or whatever it was. You even took away my fear of dancing. Why wouldn't you change me again?"

I remembered not wanting to go to the introduction, but even now I couldn't capture the feeling of resistance that I'd had, only the anger and fear that he'd taken that choice away from me.

Choices. It had seemed like I had so many, but when all roads but one were dead ends, what did a choice even mean? All I wanted was one real choice, one viable alternative. But in Dorian's world, my future had been mapped out even before I had been changed, and now there was no escape.

"I've already told you that missing the introduction simply was not an option," Dorian said. "And I thought I was helping with the dancing. I didn't mean to cause you distress." His eyes tightened at the last word. "But there are circumstances in which I think even you would call certain alterations justified."

He reached the top of the stairs and pressed a latch, and another door sprang open. I recognized his bedroom from my glimpse through the door the other day.

"I don't think so," I said, frowning up at him as he crossed the room.

"Before my research made our offer appealing to

those humans whose need was great enough to overcome the obvious risks, many agnates with objections to killing the innocent chose our candidates from among the dregs of society," Dorian said. I blinked at what seemed an abrupt change of subject. "The desperately ill, the hopelessly mad, and the criminal. Do you remember meeting Zhang Wei?"

I nodded. He was a cognate, one of the handful among the guests who weren't some admixture of European, Middle Eastern, or North African descent, and he'd shared Isabella's dead-eyed gaze.

"In his human life, he lusted after his brother's wife," he said, opening the door that led to my bedroom and carrying me through. "He seduced her or raped her—the story isn't clear, and at that time in China, there was little attention paid to the difference. When she threatened to tell her husband, he killed her children and splayed out their bodies on the marriage bed that he had defiled with her for her to find, and after she made the discovery, he attacked and killed her, too."

I shrank back in his arms. "Damn."

He continued the story. "Ling-Ling visited him the night before he was to be executed. He survived the feeding and was bonded to her. She needed him, wanted him, loved him, as she must—but he was a monster. Until she wiped all of that away."

He set me on my feet in the center of the room.

"How?" I demanded, a cold horror in the pit of my stomach. "How could she love someone who had done something like that?"

"I have killed so many more, Cora," he said sadly.

"How could you want me?"

He was right. I knew he was, but still I needed him, craved his touch, his voice, his presence. The bond was a kind of madness, but at that moment, I couldn't even want to get away, as I knew I should.

I shivered. I really was crazy.

"And what about you?" I challenged. "What if I were a doll-woman, too? Could you feel for it what you claim to feel for me?"

"Cora, I don't want you to be an Isabella," he said. "Unlike Etienne, I do not believe that is the best for you. But if some terrible accident befell you and crippled your mind or disfigured your body in a way that couldn't heal, I would not—could not—change."

There was a peculiar reassurance in that, a security that was frighteningly inviting. At the same time, how real could a feeling be if it were so completely involuntary? Could he even love, if the love wasn't based on who I was but on some strange chemical reaction? How could that be a love at all, if it didn't matter what I was? How could it be more than a compulsion?

And what did I feel for him? What name should it have? If I could call it lust and stop there, I wouldn't be so afraid.

"But you'll change me anyway," I said. "In other ways, if it's important enough to you—or if you want it badly enough, maybe you'll change me without even realizing it."

"You also change me," Dorian said, his voice low. "When we agnates are alone, the burden of existence becomes crippling. So many years, one after another, days that feel like they have been lived before, when even the hours feel used, so heavy and empty at once...."

He trailed off, then continued more matter-of-factly. "It wears on you until you chase the rush, doing anything to get a momentary thrill so that you feel, at least for a moment, alive. Or you shut out everything and everyone and slowly descend into the kind of isolation that you never come back from—the senility of the agnates is not something that is ever recoverable. The only escape for that crushing isolation is a cognate. A bond. The other, missing half. You. And the bond is never entirely one way."

Not me, I thought. *Not me, specifically, but any cognate, any girl who didn't die....*

But how many human men in the world might I fall for, if I were free from Dorian? How many chance meetings might, under the right circumstances, fill a human definition of true love?

How different was I from him, really? Did it matter that he might have bonded to another if the one he ended up with was me?

I didn't even know whether I could trust that thought, whether it was truly mine at all.

Dorian turned me away from him and untied the corset laces. This time, he worked them loose so that the hooks on the front could be slid apart. I sighed with relief as the garment dropped from my body, and he pulled me back against him for a moment and kissed the top of my head.

He released me, and I turned back around. I was

naked now except for his jewels in my ears, at my wrist and my throat. And I was increasingly aware of the wetness that was running down my leg.

I cleared my throat. "Um. If you don't mind, I need to use the bathroom."

He grinned then, an expression I'd never seen on him before. Standing there, with his hair tousled and that look on his face, he almost seemed human, as if he hadn't been confessing his own atrocities just moments before.

"Be my guest," he said. "I will join you in a minute."

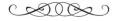

Chapter Eight

My heart sped up, and I ducked quickly into the bathroom. I should have been acutely self-conscious, I thought. I'd felt that way on Wednesday, my first time with him. And what had happened in the study had been more intimate than that, more intimate than I'd imagined possible. But now any sense of embarrassment seemed to have gone.

Could it be because he didn't want me to feel it? I tried that idea out in my mind. I didn't think so. I thought that I was changing on my own, or at least in my own response to whatever held me to him.

But it didn't matter why. Change was dangerous. He was dangerous, desperately so, a threat to everything I was or ever wanted to be. And yet when he'd grinned at me, I'd smiled back, as if he were an ordinary man. As if he didn't threaten everything I cared about.

I should be running away now, throwing on any clothes I could find and scrambling out of the window after what I had seen that night. The horror of the introduction had shown me just how bad Dorian's world could be.

But it wouldn't do any good. I could run away, escape for a day or a week, but I knew that he would eventually find me. And worse, I knew that eventually, I would walk over broken glass to get back to him. No matter what it meant to me.

As long as there was a bond between us, there was no way out.

Already, I hardly recognized my reflection. My ash brown hair was still elegant, if haphazardly so, like nothing that I'd ever worn before, and though Jane Worth's cosmetics had been smudged, they still gave an illusion of sophistication that I'd never had. A beautiful woman dripping with beautiful jewels in a beautiful house possessed by a beautiful man....

It was all so desperately, dangerously seductive, and it came with a terrible price. I took the jewelry off quickly, setting it on the counter, but the woman in the mirror looked no less strange to me.

There was a knock on the bathroom door.

I turned, my bare feet soundless on the heated marble, and stopped, my hand an inch from the knob.

Another choice that I didn't really have. Not because he'd make me but because I couldn't force myself to stop.

I opened it.

Dorian stood there, dressed in nothing but a pair of dark blue pants. I wondered why he hadn't paused to put on a shirt and shoes. Could he have wanted to see me so badly?

As badly as I now realized I wanted to see him?

I felt more naked now than I had before, shockingly naked, and I backed away hurriedly at the thrill that went through me.

His gaze raked over me, but all he said was, "If you get dressed, I'll take you home."

"Yes," I said. I'd kept backing up, and now I stood in the center of the room, a dozen feet from the door.

But I made no move toward the dressing room, where my clothes waited for me.

After a long moment in which neither of us moved, he shut the door and hit a button near it. A low hum indicated that a fan had come on somewhere.

"Heat," he said, catching the question in my expression.

We were going to go. Go away, go to my apartment, where he would leave me alone. That's what I wanted. It had to be, because this craziness, the lust and the ache and all the things I didn't want to name, they were all a lie.

But I couldn't look away from his eyes, searching them, as if they held the secrets of my own soul.

And I said, "Dorian, I can't. Please don't make me."

At those words, he rocked on his toes, and a muscle in his jaw spasmed. The night he'd found me freezing on the road, I'd hit him with all my strength, and he hadn't even flinched. But now my words made his entire body sway.

Oh, God. What had I done. What was I doing....

"A little while," he said. "Just an hour longer. And then you have to promise me that you'll go."

"Okay." I was ready to agree to almost anything.

"Okay," he repeated, and he smiled then, but his eyes looked like something was broken inside.

He crossed to the shower, the transition to which was marked by an arched frameless glass enclosure flush against the basket-weave floor. After tapping on the touch screen on the wall next to the opening, he reached in and manipulated several of the imposing array of chrome knobs and buttons, and water sheeted down like rain from a series of panels in the ceiling as steam rose up to frost the glass.

He extended his hand wordlessly, and I approached, hesitant in spite of my own plea to stay. My body drew tight with awareness of the nearness of him.

I put my hand in his.

He drew me close, his face serious, his eyes shadowed, but all he said was, "Your hair is still up. More or less."

Without invitation, Dorian began plucking bobby pins from my tousled chignon, dropping them carelessly to the floor. The look in his eyes turned the impersonal action into a caress, and the glorious mess that Jane had created slipped downward until it fell in a mass of waves to just brush my nipples, which hardened at the touch. Dorian's wicked smile returned, and my heart sped up.

Tiny goose bumps rose on my scalp as his fingers searched through my hair for any fasteners that he had missed, and his fingers felt so good, so right in my hair.

"Come here," Dorian said, hooking an arm around me and pulling me against his body. I obeyed, a little breathless, melting against his strength.

He took my mouth, and I reveled in the insistent demand of his lips and tongue. I felt him harden through the fabric of his pants. An answering ache bloomed between my thighs.

Dorian broke off the kiss. He stepped backward into the sheeting water and pulled me with him, tugging the shower door closed after us.

The shower was warm enough to startle a small yelp from me—I'd become more chilled than I realized, standing naked in the bathroom. But after just a moment, my skin adjusted, and muscles I had not realized were tight began to loosen under the warm, steady wash. The styling products that had kept my hair in place began to flow down into my face, and I screwed my eyes shut and scraped my hair back.

I opened my eyes to catch Dorian looking keenly down at me, water running off the flawless planes of his face.

"Your clothes," I said reaching out to the waistband of his soaked pants.

He just reached between us and unfastened his pants, peeling off the clinging fabric and flinging it into a corner of the shower.

"Better?" he asked, catching an arm around my waist and pulling me against him. We were front-to-front, and his hardness pressed between our bellies. The strangeness of it, of everything, hit me again.

"I can't believe I'm here," I blurted. "Doing this." I'd wanted to do this. I'd chosen to do this, asked to do it. What was wrong with me? "My friends—they would freak out. They'd kill me. They'd kill you, some rich old pervert taking advantage of an undergrad."

He caught the nape of my neck and bent his head down to mine, nuzzling against my cheek before brushing his lips to mine.

I shivered and shut my eyes, leaning into him.

"And what would you tell them?" he asked softly.

"I don't know. I still don't know what this is," I admitted. "It's not like anything I ever expected." I opened my eyes and pulled back to look at him squarely. "Or wanted."

His hands slipped over my water-slick body, one on my back, the other cupping my rear and pulling me more firmly against him. My skin flamed with awareness where he touched me.

"But you want it now." It was not a question.

"Yes," I breathed. *Oh, yes. For as long as he was with me, I would want this—and when we were apart, I would ache for it. It was the bond, had to be the bond.*

"This isn't something your friends can understand." He kissed my neck, and I shivered as my knees weakened slightly.

"But I don't understand it, either," I protested. Who could? I'd known this man—this half-devil, half-angel—for scarcely more than a month. If I didn't count the time I spent unconscious, I had spent time with him only over seven days. At the third, he'd transported me out of my body, taken my blood because I had given it to him and in return had presented me with a new life. I'd let him do it, wanted him to do it more than I had ever wanted anything. At our forth meeting, I'd tumbled into bed with him, and now, at our seventh, he'd proceeded to frighten me beyond my imagining with the terrible society of his people. Yet I was here again, in his arms.

And I couldn't want to be anywhere else.

His voice was low in my ear. "You will understand, Cora. We have all the time you need."

His head dipped to my shoulder, and I leaned back against the cool shower wall as his mouth and the water moved over me, letting the sensations carry me away. The heat was back, the thrumming need that started deep in my womb and lanced along my nerves, into my clit, my nipples, my lips, following his mouth and making me hurt with desire.

Dorian cupped a hand with the lower edge against my breast, holding it away so that the shower ran to fill it up, the trickling edge of water teasing at my nipple. He caressed the hard nub with his thumb through the warmth of the water, and I shivered.

He kissed a line between my breasts, kneeling to lavish my hips and navel with attention. The image of him, on his knees before me, burned into my brain and shook me as much as the feel of his mouth on my body did.

Dorian rose up again to take my other nipple into his mouth, stroking and pulling it into a peak so hard that the juncture of my thighs ached. I grabbed his hair, unable to stop myself, my breath hissing through my teeth.

His hand slipped between us, and he cupped my mound and entrance in one hand, unmoving for a long moment as his mouth tortured first one breast and then the other, the water sheeting down over us.

Then he slid two fingers in to their limit, and I gasped at the friction at my entrance. He half withdrew them to find the place—*that* place—that had pushed me into climax before. My body knew what was coming next and tightened in response.

"Please," I said, not even sure whether I meant for him to do it or to spare me—not because I didn't want it but because I was afraid of what pieces of myself I'd leave behind when I came.

He pressed against it, and I shuddered in his arms. His thumb was still on my mound, and he clasped me, inside and out, rhythmically tightening and loosening his grasp as his mouth continued its assault on my self-control. I spiraled up and up, rocking with him until I went crashing sideways into the heat of another orgasm, my skin so hot that the water felt like ice, my legs giving way so that he had to slip his free arm around me and hold me up, against him.

The waves receded, and I was left, limp and panting, in his arms as he looked down at me, his eyes so dark with desire that the blue had retreated to a thin line around the well of blackness.

"Turn around," he said, setting me on my feet and turning me so that I faced the shower wall.

Water poured across my too-sensitive skin.

"Lean forward," he ordered. "More."

I whimpered as I obeyed, remembering the closet—wanting that again, the force and the urgency and, yes, the edge of pain. I felt thin, pulled to the limit. The marble wall was blessedly cool against my forearms, a welcome counterpoint to the torture of the water.

He nudged my legs apart with his, and I felt him step between them, urging me wider. One hand gripped my hip, and I braced myself. I felt the hard head slide up my thigh, and other hand was between my thighs, opening me and guiding his erection into me.

I gasped as he entered—the head pressed against the place that his hand had just taken to acute sensitivity. I marveled at the sense of being invaded and filled, so alien and intimate, satisfying a void that I hadn't even known existed a week ago. He held me there, against the shower wall, thrust in so deep so that I could feel the nest of hair at the base pressing against my buttocks, the root of him hard against my entrance. The stillness of him was a torment.

His hand slid up along my folds and between my buttocks, brushing the place behind my entrance where I stretched to accommodate him and skimming up, sending a jolt over me as he brushed over my hip and back down my belly to roll my clit lightly in his fingers.

By then I was panting with my need for him to move inside of me, squirming ineffectually as he held me still against him with his other hand.

"Tell me what you want, Cora," he ordered.

He ordered, but there was no force behind it. As if

he wanted me to sign my own fate.

"Dorian," I protested.

"Dorian, what?" His fingers tortured me, making me throb around him.

"Do it," I groaned. "Do *me.*" And I couldn't say the other thoughts that crowded up in my brain, that I wanted the edge, the danger, and oh, please, the pain....

I didn't know whether he realized what I wanted or had obeyed his own desires, but his fingers dug into my hips. My face shoved into my arms on the wall of the shower, his body slick with water against mine as he drove in hard. It hurt against my swollen, over-tender flesh, but I wanted all of it, I welcomed it, wanted more of everything, the pain and pleasure bleeding one into another.

He gave it to me, launching me hard into the grips of an orgasm that came tearing through me, tearing me apart, and I welcomed myself flying apart. My knees began to buckle as I slid away.

"Stand up, Cora," he hissed.

I did, forcing my knees to lock, and the effort trapped me in my body even as my climax battered me. I could feel the ragged breaths in my chest, the contractions of my innermost parts around the hardness of him, the shuddering, glorious electricity that pulsed with it in my clit and nipples, the tingling surges that rippled down into my arms and to my feet, planted firmly against the shower floor.

The contractions weakened, weakened to a quivering shadow of what they had been, and still he thrust into to me, again and again until I pressed my flushed face against the shower wall and he came in a great shudder that overtook his powerful frame. I closed my eyes as he filled me, feeling the pumping of his balls against the back of my thighs.

I welcomed that, too, and took it as my due. And then he said my name, and I almost came undone again.

A minute later, he withdrew and turned me, pulling me into his embrace and kissing me again and again. He reached for a container of body wash—not mine, because my own shower things were still on the deck of the tub—flipped it open with one hand, inverted it and squeezed it onto my belly, rubbing it across me before the shower could wash it away. His palm caressed my neck, my breasts, and slid down to wash between my folds.

I caught my breath as his fingers explored them, efficiently and thoroughly.

"You're enjoying this," I said, half an accusation.

"Completely," he agreed, his hand sluicing water over my buttocks, his fingertips brushing up the crease in my buttocks so that I shivered and turned my face into his chest.

"I will have that, too, in time," he said, the words a promise. "And you will give it to me. Gladly."

CHAPTER NINE

His hands moved up my back then, caressing the red marks, already healing, on my hips and moving up to my shoulder blades under my hair.

There were no lines of my making, I thought. The only limits were his. Each time we were together, he pushed me a little farther. I denied him nothing—and I never would.

The end would be wherever he decided. And I knew it would be far beyond anything I would choose.

He stepped away and retrieved a bottle of shampoo, and the thoughts fell away. They were so slippery in his presence, my fears too hard to hold onto. And that was, perhaps, the most frightening thing of all.

"That's girly stuff," I said, distracting myself as Dorian poured a dollop of shampoo into his hand.

"This is your bathroom," he said. "What do you expect it to be?"

He motioned at me to turn away. Heating with the memory of what had happened the last time I'd done so, I obeyed. He began to massage the shampoo through my hair, and I tipped back my head so that it would run down my back and not into my eyes.

"So you even picked out a shampoo for me?" I asked, some part of my bitterness seeping into my voice.

"Worth did. But she'll buy whatever brand you desire," he said evenly, his fingers moving through my hair. "She couldn't predict what you would like."

I felt a small twinge of relief at that—and then an even smaller echo of horror that I had reached the point of fearing that even my choice of soap would be taken away.

"So she defaulted to Fekkai?" I asked lightly, covering my reaction.

I could hear the smile in his voice. "Only the best."

"Did she buy them after you...we...the bond happened?" I finished lamely. "Like the clothes? That seems quick."

His fingers stilled in my hair for a moment, then resumed their motion. "This room has been ready for you since before you were born," he said quietly. "Once every two years, the toiletries are replaced. Every ten years, I order it to be redecorated. Every twenty, the bath is remodeled."

Again, I was reminded of how I had stepped into a

place that had been waiting for the right person to fill it. All those years, lying empty, waiting for Dorian to find a cognate. And then I came, only to try to reject everything. I insisted that I would continue my old life at the university, and the future that had been laid out for me, so neatly, so long ago, would sit unused.

But would it? Already, I'd asked to stay—for the night, maybe, but how hard would it be to stay for another and then another? To stay with Dorian, to let myself be spoiled and pampered, to wear the beautiful clothes and claim the great, cold mansion as my own.... How long would it be before I gave up any pretense of maintaining my old life?

How long would it be before I gave up my innermost self?

I stood silently as he worked conditioner through my hair and finished cleaning my legs and feet. He turned me back to face him and, with a soft cloth, washed the remnants of makeup from my face, punctuating his actions with kisses that sent small tremors of sensation through me. I giggled involuntarily as he plucked the individual false eyelashes from my eyes and dropped them to the shower floor.

"Still like what you see with the mask gone?" I quipped.

He looked down at me, the quirk of his lips sad. "You have no idea."

My breath felt tight in my chest. But what other answer could he give?

He dropped the cloth onto the shower shelf a moment later. "There's a towel on the warmer on the wall," he said—permission and an invitation in one.

"I know. I found it two nights ago," I said. A fresh one had replaced it each morning.

I stepped out of the shower and wrapped myself in the thick, toasty bath sheet that went nearly to my ankles. I looked back at the shower. Dorian was soaping up under the shower panels. Girly products or no, it was a sight to behold. Tearing my eyes away, I passed into the chilly dressing room and flicked on the light.

I opened a drawer in one of the low built-ins. My hands lingered over the froths of lace and silk, but I put on the plain cotton hip-huggers and the t-shirt bra I'd packed. Then I went to the hanging section of the closet to dig between the Marc Jacobs and BCBG. Even the fabric of the designer clothes was heavier and softer, and next to them, my own clothes looked worn, shabby. I pulled them on anyway. I couldn't say yes even to a t-shirt, because once I started saying yes, I didn't know that I would ever stop.

When I returned to the bathroom, I had a pang of disappointment to discover that Dorian was gone, and the disappointment sent a second, more sinister pang through me—one of fear.

I shouldn't care. I shouldn't want. I shouldn't crave. If I couldn't resist him, there was no hope for me.

The jewelry still sat on the counter where I had left it, the emerald pieces and the ruby teardrop pendant that was secured to the center of the necklace. Dorian had given it to me—a Christmas present, he had said. I unhooked it from the necklace and held it in my hand. It was the twin to the mark on my wrist, the mark of our bond.

"Cora."

I closed my fingers around the pendant and looked up.

Dorian was standing in the doorway between the bedroom and the bathroom, wearing a plain white dress shirt, open at the throat, and a sports coat.

"Ready to go?" he asked.

Reflexively, I shoved the pendant into my pocket. I still didn't want to leave, but I wanted to wish to leave. And in that convoluted state, I knew I had to go, or I risked losing even more of myself than I had already given.

"Are you sure it's safe?" I asked instead of admitting any of that.

"It's as safe as it ever will be," he said.

So. Home—or hide in his shadow forever.

I knew I had to choose home.

I nodded and came out of the door to join him in the bedroom, grabbing my keys, wallet, and phone and stuffing them into my pockets with the pendant. Dorian opened the door onto the mezzanine and waited for me to pass though, looping his arm over my shoulder as I went by.

It was disturbing how good it felt there. Like it belonged.

"Do I have a secret staircase, too?" I asked to distract myself from that thought as we passed by the door to his bedroom.

He smiled. "It's a servant's stair, and yes, there is one to your bedroom that leads from the drawing room to a hidden door."

"Drawing room? Really?" I looked askance at the archaic name.

He chuckled. "You can call it the keeping room or the family room if it makes you feel better. It's off the dining room."

"Do you have a billiards room, too?"

"Of course," he said as we reached the head of the stairs and started down. "And a library, a music room, several parlors, a breakfast room, conservatory...."

"Miss Scarlett in the conservatory with the candle-stick," I quipped.

"Pardon?"

"Never mind." It still all seemed so unreal. "When did you buy this monstrosity?"

He looked down at me, an inscrutable expression flickering over his face. "I designed it, Cora, modeled somewhat after a palazzo in Tuscany that Palladio designed for me."

I let out a puff of air, deflated.

"I forget," I said. "I know, but at the same time.... I must seem like such a child to you."

"All humans do. I can't remember being as young as a human. *Thinking* as young as any human." He shook his head.

"How can this work, then?" I asked, my mind re-volving inevitably back to the bond that was between us. "You. Me. Everything."

"It just will, Cora." He raked his fingers through his still-damp hair. "Do you think you're the only one to change?"

We arrived in the foyer. I could hear, faintly, the sound of the orchestra still playing below, and the butler materialized with my jacket and a long wool coat for Dorian. I shrugged mine on.

"You just accept everything. How can you do that?" I demanded.

His gaze was piercing. "Not everything. But I don't reject happiness just because it doesn't match my expectations."

Dorian turned away at that, striding out the door that the butler held open, and I was left to follow in his wake.

Happiness. What he offered me wasn't happiness. It was a bondage of the mind. If I couldn't feel anything except contentment, that contentment couldn't be real.

Could it?

The courtyard garden was blanketed with snow, only the flagstone walk swept bare. The low boxwoods were white hillocks, and the snow was still coming down, flakes slipping around the neck of my jacket to melt against my skin.

Dorian stalked between the walls of holly. When I passed through, I saw the car at the curb and stopped.

"What is that?" I asked. It was all angles and edges, a dark color that seemed to suck in the light.

"Lamborghini Murciélago," he said, swinging open the passenger door. He treated me to a narrow look. "It means 'bat.'"

"Subtle, as usual," I said, ducking in. He shut the door. The seat was narrower than those in the Bentley, with a wide, complicated-looking console between the driver and passenger.

I looked at Dorian as he swung in, a thought striking me. "Vampires can't really...I mean, real ones...."

"No, agnates cannot transform into bats," he said dryly, "any more than we turn into dust in sunlight or at the touch of holy water. Another human myth."

"I didn't think you did," I said a little stiffly. "I just wanted to make sure."

"Hmm," he said, a smile playing at the edges of his lips, and I realized that I'd been baited as he pulled away from the curb, the car leaping forward at the lightest touch.

This new side of Dorian, this lighter side, always took me by surprise. It would appear from nowhere, then disappear as quickly as a rock dropped into a pond.

"I have another question," I said.

"Yes?"

"It's about the woman with two cognates."

"Veronica." Even in the streetlight, the disapproval was clear on Dorian's face.

"Her," I agreed. "The other agnates didn't seem to like her very much."

"Even the more depraved currents among agnatic society believe that it is not in good taste to continue killing when one already has a cognate, if for no other reason than because you might take a cognate that perhaps could have bonded to another," Dorian said.

"But she did it."

"Veronica enjoys flaunting our customs."

"It's possible, I mean."

"Very possible," he agreed as he took a turn

smoothly onto New Hampshire.

"Does that mean that if Etienne had bitten me, I would have bonded to him, instead?"

He shrugged. "No one knows. No one can know. With my research, I've been able to determine that most humans will never bond to any agnate, no matter what the circumstances. But though I hope to narrow the one-in-one-hundred further, it appears that there are factors at play that cannot be accounted for by mere blood compatibility—which means that no human could bond to every agnate."

"So we might really be made for each other," I said. "Sort of."

He kept his gaze fixed on the road. "It seems more and more likely. It can't be tested directly, though, even if anyone would risk it. Once you're bonded to one agnate, you can never be bonded to another."

"Do you still want to, you know, bite other people?" I asked hesitantly. "Like, other human women?"

"No," he said flatly. "Veronica does it just because she can."

"And when she bonded again?" I pursued. "What does she feel for her second cognate?"

"It is a bond," he said simply. "So she feels the same toward both."

"Love?" I said dubiously.

"I don't know that she is capable of love," he said. "But whatever she can feel, she feels equally."

I looked up at his face, all shadows and highlights in the streetlights. His face had settled back into the impassive expression that he usually wore—no more open smiles, no soft glances. It made my heart ache, and I tried not to think about why.

"And you?" I asked, speaking before I could stop myself. "Are you capable of loving someone?"

He turned to look at me. "To the ends of the earth."

I bit my lip and hugged myself, hard.

CHAPTER TEN

When we arrived at the University of Maryland, Dorian pulled into the parking lot instead of stopping at the curb outside my apartment building. In response to my quizzical look, he just motioned to a scrap of paper on the dashboard and said, "I'll walk you up. I have a daily permit."

Uncomfortably, I remembered that Geoff, my human not-quite-boyfriend, had said something similar only a week—and a lifetime—before.

Geoff. What was I going to do about Geoff? I looked at Dorian, and I couldn't seem to even keep the two of them in my mind at the same time.

He parked, and I popped open my door automatically as he was still circling the car. Dorian caught the door and closed it after me. He extended his hand, and after a moment's hesitation, I took it, the familiar thrill going through me, and we began walking toward the building.

It was strange, him being there. It seemed wrong. Dorian belonged to his top-floor Baltimore office and his great old house in Georgetown. He didn't belong here, on the College Park campus, stepping up onto the sidewalks I traveled every day to class.

I wasn't sure if it was because Dorian was too real for the university or the university was too real for him. Either way, I was feeling my worlds collide, and it definitely wasn't comfortable.

It hadn't hit me the other day when we'd come here with Clarissa and I'd packed a bag to take back to Dorian's mansion. Maybe the paparazzi djinn lurking in a parallel dimension had something to do with it. That day had been too chaotic and confusing, a madness that had begun the day before with the attempt on my life.

I swiped my access card to get into the building and hit the button for the fourth floor. We stepped into the elevator, and I let it rise in silence. There he was, Dorian, my vampire, standing in the elevator to my apartment. And this time, I had all but invited him.

What had I gotten myself into?

I pulled my hand from his and led the way down the hall, taking my key from my pocket to unlock the door. The apartment was chilly and dark. Even after I flipped on the light, the emptiness of it, of the building, seemed more than I could fill.

My apartment had once been a sanctuary, the closest thing I had to home since I had to clean out Gramma's house to get it ready to sell. But the last time I had been alone on campus, a djinn had nearly killed me. Now the walls and locks seemed no more secure than if they'd been made of tissue paper.

I turned to face Dorian. He stood in the hall, as poised as always, impossibly handsome and utterly inhuman. He had no place in my world, with its tests and movie marathons and microwaved meals. If I was going to keep my life, I had no room for him.

Now was the time when I should send him home, back to the great mausoleum of a house where he belonged, buried in his wealth and antiquities. Buried in his memories.

I opened my mouth, and what came out instead was, "Want to come in?"

He arched an eyebrow. "Of course."

I stood back to let him in, and I knew that he'd be staying the night. I was probably breaking half a dozen terms of my lease, but then again, there weren't many rules left that Christina and Chelsea hadn't already shattered.

I shut the door after him and pulled off my coat, hanging it on one of the self-stick wall hooks we'd put behind the door. I held out my hand for his, and he gave it over. Even his jacket didn't look right, hanging on my wall.

I cleared my throat. "If you didn't notice before, this one's my bathroom. In case you need to use it."

I opened the door into the small, utilitarian room, cluttered with Lisette's bottles of products.

"Lisette and I share it, actually," I said.

Vampires did use the bathroom, didn't they? I thought. Immediately, I chided myself. They ate, drank, and had sex. Of course they used the bathroom. How was it that after everything, Dorian still seemed impossible enough to me that I even had that question? It was almost as if I was afraid of him being real.

Heading toward the living area, I led him past the door of my bedroom, which was the only one standing open.

"Yours," he said, reaching past me and flicking on the light.

"You should know," I said, crossing my arms over my chest as I turned to face him. "You sent your people to clean it."

I hadn't let him into my bedroom…before. Even now, it was an intimacy I wasn't fully prepared for.

Dorian was the last person I should have in here with me now, even if he was one of the few who might be able to help against a djinn.

If I'm that scared, I should have gotten him to call Clarissa. Maybe she'd find it amusing to hang out on a college campus for the night.

But I didn't want her. I wanted Dorian.

Because I was an idiot.

Self-consciously, I surveyed my crowded bedroom, taking in the extra dresser, the bed with its double-stacked twin mattresses, and the cinderblocks I had used to raise it so I could cram everything I had boxed up from Gramma's house underneath it.

"Princess and the pea?" Dorian asked, nodding to

the extra mattress and box springs.

I hugged myself. "A few of my Gramma's things and the stuff from my room at home. She died last year, and I don't really have the money for a storage unit. I'm really not a hoarder, but I don't have anywhere else to put it right now."

And then his face opened, like a curtain being lifted, and I saw sympathy written there.

"I didn't know, Cora, or I wouldn't have teased," he said softly. "I'm sorry about your grandmother. Your medical records listed no next-of-kin, but I didn't have any idea what that meant."

"I thought you'd have gone to the effort of finding out something like that," I said around the sudden lump in my throat. It was stupid, but seeing the room with fresh eyes made the old wound ache. It looked...sad.

"I didn't look too deeply into the pasts of candidates," he said.

Because almost all of them would die. And the less he knew, the less he would have to remember—or to forget.

I could have died. By sheer odds, even with the screening, I should have died. The paths I had, the future he'd set for me and the one I had wanted for myself, would have been moot then.

But I survived. And now it seemed like the harder I clung to my past, the faster it slipped away.

"I'm not a candidate anymore, though," I said. "I haven't been for more than a week. You didn't care enough to find out about my family since then?"

Dorian's forehead creased. "I don't remember

mine."

I blinked. "You don't remember what?"

"My mother. My father. I don't remember them. I don't know if I had any brothers or sisters." He was still looking at me, but I had the sense that he wasn't seeing me at all. "I know that my parents loved me very much, and sometimes I think I remember a smell, a snatch of song...."

He broke off and shook his head. "Perhaps. Or perhaps I just remember myself, trying to remember."

"Oh," I said. I didn't remember mine, but that was because they'd died as I was born. But Gramma had been my family, and I couldn't imagine forgetting her.

That was almost worse than the idea that he didn't care—the idea that he didn't think that things like parents and grandmothers were worth knowing about. The idea that they were just another fact, another circumstance, that would become irrelevant in time.

"You look sad for me," he said. "Don't be, Cora. I'm content enough now."

Now. With me, or with his victory against his political opponents? God, was I being unfair? Did I care if I was?

He took my chin and kissed me gently, and I closed my eyes, clinging to him, as the sweet warmth trickled through my body.

"Why did you invite me in, Cora?" he asked softly when he pulled away.

"Because I'm scared," I admitted. "I know you say it's safe, but you didn't think I was in danger before."

"There are no guarantees in the world," Dorian

admitted. "The longer I live, the more I know this is true. But I also know that living in fear is only half living."

"And I want you to try to understand my world, too," I added, realizing that it was true only as I said the words. "I don't have a great big house or a ton of mystery or some great load of money or fabulous talent or...really, anything. I'm a college student. I live in a dorm apartment. I do college student things. And I'm sure that to you, it seems like a small and unimportant life, but maybe if you see just a little more of it, you can understand why it's the life I want."

"I'm a patient man, Cora. If this is what you want right now, I won't stand in your way." He stood in the doorway, my boring, ordinary doorway, and it did nothing to diminish him.

I shook my head. He said those words, but everything that had happened that night had shown only too clearly that my old life couldn't survive the new one. My plans had no room for Dorian in them—and Dorian's world had no room for me. Not really. It had a place for the cognate I was supposed to become.

I didn't bother arguing with him. I knew it would get nowhere—resolve nothing, because nothing could be resolved. Not as long as I was bonded to him.

"There was one other reason," I said instead.

"Yes?" he prompted.

"I don't want to be alone." There. I'd said it. "Not tonight. I've spent too many nights alone and scared, knowing that I was dying. I don't want to be alone again tonight."

He closed the space between us so quickly that I had no time to react before he was gathering me in his arms.

"Oh, Cora," he said. "You never have to be alone again."

And I didn't know whether I was more relieved or afraid.

CHAPTER ELEVEN

I woke up the next morning wearing nothing but Dorian's body wrapped around mine. Pushing my fears back to sleep, I savored the sensation for a long time, his arm draped over my waist, his breath against the back of my neck, my butt snugged against his stomach and the slight sleeping erection there.

Then my bladder woke up, too, and made its ordinary demands clearly known. I disengaged myself as carefully as I could, trying not to wake him, but he roused immediately.

"Good morning, beautiful," he said, his eyes still soft with sleep.

Damn, but he was breathtaking, this man in my bed who claimed too much of me.

"I think that was my line," I returned, clambering rather gracelessly over him before sliding to the ground. I grabbed a t-shirt and panties and headed for the bathroom. When I finished and opened the door, I found Dorian waiting outside of it, wearing only his boxer briefs.

"Your turn," I said, ducking under his arm.

He came out as I was pouring a bowl of Cheerios, dressed in the white shirt and dress pants from the night before. He dropped his blazer on the counter.

He looked like he belonged in the apartment now. I wasn't sure whether that should reassure me or disturb me more, so I chose to be reassured. Either way, there wasn't much I could do about it.

"Help yourself," I said, swinging open the door to the cabinet where the bowls and cereal were kept. "I don't have a fully staffed kitchen to make me a buffet every morning, but I muddle through somehow."

"That was for your benefit, since the chef couldn't predict what you would like," Dorian said, stepping into the narrow aisle between the cabinets. "If you communicate with the kitchen the night before, they'll cook to order."

"Oh, well, how practical," I said, shaking my head as he entirely missed my point.

He chose the raisin bran and filled a bowl. I couldn't help but smirk as I watched him.

"What is it?" he asked, too observant, as always.

"You. I mean, you're like a thousand years old, and you're eating raisin bran for breakfast." I hopped up onto the counter and dug in.

"And what exactly am I supposed to have for breakfast, being 'like a thousand years old?'" he asked, putting the milk back in the fridge.

"I don't know," I said. "Something more exciting than that."

"There have been many times in my life when a bowl of cereal would have been far more exciting than what I had," he said dryly. He leaned against the stove across from me and scooped up a spoonful of raisin bran.

"I thought you were super-rich," I retorted.

He shrugged, looking amused. "I've been wealthy much more of my life than I haven't. It isn't hard when you live a long time and are very, very persuasive, at least as far as humans are concerned."

"Persuasive? Like, 'Give me all your money' persuasive?"

His expression grew clouded. "It is more a matter of holding on to what I've earned in the face of adversity. But you can't eat gold or property, and agnates have no powers to tell the future. It's easy to become jaded, complacent. When you live in a city that has flourished virtually unmolested for three hundred years, it's easy to see the last invader—the one destined to pull it to the ground—as just another minor inconvenience in a history of prosperity. The next thing you know, the fields are burnt, the livestock gone, and the countryside filled with a hostile army."

"That sounds bad," I said. I knew he was describing his own past, impossibly distant from anything I'd ever experienced.

I took another bite of my cereal. It tasted like cardboard.

I added, "I think we have a bit of a generation gap, here. Like, a ten-generation gap."

His expression was unusually gentle. "We'll have plenty of time for us to build our own history."

I tried to imagine a day when I could think like him—when I could look back on three or four centuries and talk about the decade I realized that the decay of the United States was irreversible or that some new super-power was going to launch the world into war. I shook my head. It seemed impossible, but even then, I would be no more than a child to him.

How could any relationship be built on that, even if I wanted it to be?

"What do you study here?" Dorian asked abruptly.

I blinked. "I thought you didn't care."

"You care. Perhaps I should care. Perhaps it's a thing like grandmothers—something I have forgotten to care about."

There was a lot more going on behind those clear blue eyes than I had given him credit for. For all my questions, all I ever thought about was what he wanted from me, what he did to me, what my life meant to him in the context of his history. I'd wondered the night before if he even peed—because I still didn't credit him with being fully real.

"Economics," I said, as awkward as any first date. "I want to go to grad school, then work for a govern-mental agency or maybe a nonprofit, studying markets. After I got sick, I was thinking maybe healthcare."

"I have any number of businesses. I'm sure that some of them make use of economists," Dorian said.

Was he really offering what I thought he was? "I don't need you to find me a job."

"A job. A company." He shrugged. "Whatever you wish."

"I've worked for everything I have," I objected. "I've earned my scholarship and my grades, and I'm going to earn my degree. I don't need to be given a job—or a company."

"It's not about need. I want you to have it," he said mildly.

My mind rebelled. When someone could come in and drop into my lap so much more than I'd ever hoped to earn, it made my own efforts seem pitiful in comparison.

Did that mean I was proud of standing on my own two feet? Or was I just too easily ashamed of how little I'd been able to do?

"Think about it. The offer stands," Dorian continued. "Don't want a corporation? How about a charity? Feed the starving children of whatever country you wish."

And that offer struck me like a knife in the heart. How did I dare say no to that? All it would cost was my own small life, and how many others could I save? And I'd have happiness…of a sort. Eventually. Dorian would see to that.

"What if I want to go to grad school?" I didn't realize I'd spoken those words until I heard them. My own small, selfish dream. Would he give me that?

Dorian blinked. For once, I'd surprised him. "Yes, you'd said something about that. The University of Maryland has an excellent program—"

"I didn't apply to UMD. It's not one of my choices."

Dorian was quiet for a long moment. "The research labs are here, Cora. And at this moment, the world's politics revolve around Washington, and I'm in the center of them."

"Right," I said. "That's what I thought."

"I didn't say no," he said.

"You didn't have to." He wouldn't leave D.C. And I couldn't stand to be away from him for a whole week at a time. After only twenty-four hours, I could hardly think of anything but him.

"We can work something out," he said, but I couldn't imagine what. "In the more immediate future, I want you to consider coming to my New Year's Eve party."

"Will it be like the Lesser Introduction?" I asked. I didn't bother to hide my distaste.

"No. I will not subject you to that again. You've seen the gamut of our society. I want you to see the best of it now. I want you to see what's worth fighting for."

I looked at him over my bowl of cereal. "What if I say no? Will you force me again?"

He had that weary look again, the one I couldn't quite understand. "This is not an obligation that I must keep, nor is it something that must be done to keep you safe. If you refuse, I won't make you come. But I want you to give me a chance to show you what else a bond can mean."

I thought about testing him then, refusing just to find out if he was telling the truth about not making me.

But he was right—if there was something better than what the night before had shown me, I should see it. I wanted to, and I was sure it was me wanting, not him. I needed some sign of light beyond the trust in him that the bond had forced on me.

I looked up at him where he stood across from me. In the utilitarian kitchen, his appearance was even more striking. Jarring, even. And he wanted me—more of me than I had ever expected to give to anyone.

Did I even want to refuse him?

"I'll come," I said.

He nodded with satisfaction and took the single step to the sink, where he washed his bowl and spoon, dried them, and put them away. I took the last bite of my cereal, and he held out his hand. I gave my own bowl and spoon over and watched as he repeated the process.

I was struck again with an almost dizzying sense of his immediacy, his tangibility, the water running over his too-perfect hands as they moved the sponge efficiently over the earthenware.

"I could clean your toilets as well, if that would interest you as much," he said dryly.

I jumped a little guiltily. "Can you read my mind?" I wouldn't put anything past him.

He raised his hand to brush his damp knuckles against my cheek, and I shivered. I would never get used to that touch.

"No," he said. "But I don't have to. Sometimes your thoughts are written on your face. I can, however, feel echoes of any particularly strong emotion that you have."

I thought of how much I had missed him on Christmas morning when I had woken alone. "So when we were apart...." I began.

"I didn't have to feel you then to know what you were feeling, Cora. I felt myself." Again, that sad smile.

And he would be leaving again soon. Because I would insist on it. I had to insist on it, to keep my own mind, my sanity apart from him. To put some semblance of a barrier between the parts of my life.

He had stepped between my knees where I perched on the edge of the counter, his eyes almost level with mine. I watched his expression change, growing more intent.

Did he sense how desperately I wanted him to stay? How desperately I wanted him to touch me, in spite of everything?

Involuntarily, I leaned forward, tipped my head up, and he bent to catch my mouth. I sank into the kiss, wishing I could disappear into it, just for a moment, and forget everything.

My abdomen clenched, a twinge of anticipation wakening my body, sensitizing it to his touch. He pulled me to him. I looped my arms around his neck, kissing him back hard, not content this time to merely be stroked by him. My tongue pushed past his teeth, into his mouth, tasting him, wanting him to be a part of me as I wanted to be a part of him. His hands were under my shirt, against my naked flesh.

My nipples tightened at the stroke of his thumb, heightening the need between my legs. My blood sang with it, my head light and hot at once. I ground my hips against the hardness that bulged at his fly, panting against his mouth. His fingers slid beneath the elastic of my panties. Hooking my legs around him, I kissed his neck as he traced the edge of the elastic down to just beside my entrance, urging him on with my mouth, tasting his skin and wanting more.

His fingers slid sideways, between my folds. I made a strangled sound. He stroked me slowly, holding me against his hand as he dipped shallowly, teasingly into my entrance, coming up to rhythmically roll the root of my clit between his thumb and forefinger while I shuddered in his arms. He pushed me right to the edge of an orgasm, but he held me back, until my entire body felt so suffused that I thought I could stand it no longer.

"Dorian," I managed.

I felt both his hands at one hip, then a sudden ripping noise, which he repeated on the other side. My panties dropped away—he had torn them from my body.

Even in my befuddled state, I felt a surge of outrage. "What—?"

"I'll buy you more," he said, his hands at his fly.

That wasn't the point, but I was in no position to argue it at that moment. A moment later, Dorian was holding me again, smothering whatever protest I might have managed with another kiss.

His hand, still damp from stroking me, slid between the counter and my buttocks, then up, to my entrance again, where his fingers resumed the maddening rhythm that pushed me right to the edge again.

My hands tightened into fists in his hair as I strained to reach climax.

"Tell me how much you want it," he said, his voice rough and low in my ear.

"You know, dammit," I said.

He just gave his wicked laugh and looped his arms under my knees pulling my ankles up over his shoulders. Then, slipping his fingers inside of me, he hooked against that sensitive place, and with his thumb against my clitoris, he took me up and over.

Without losing the rhythm, he withdrew his fingers and thrust himself deep inside me, and the first spasms of my orgasm were launched into something far more intense. His wet fingers worked my clitoris as he drove into me, the contractions wringing my body in time to his movements. His other arm held me against him even as my own arms loosened uselessly.

I felt him shudder just at the last surge receded as his release came after mine. For a long moment, I just clung to him as he held me, feeling his heart beating through the thickness of our shirts, his breath in my hair, the strength of his arms around me.

I realized I never wanted him to leave. And it scared me.

With every ounce of will, I let go of him, my body protesting its reluctance with an almost physical pain.

"I need you to go," I said. "Before I ask you to stay." Or before I asked him to take me back with him to that beautiful, dangerous house and the place that was made just for someone like me....

He stepped back, his eyes hooded, and adjusted his pants. "You'll find a way to be at peace in your own mind, Cora."

"Because I have to?" I asked.

"Because you will want to," he said.

He pressed his lips against my cheek, and I closed my eyes, just breathing him for a long moment. And then he was gone.

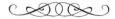

CHAPTER TWELVE

I let out a breath. The apartment seemed smaller and dingier, somehow, and I had to fight the urge to go running out half-naked after him.

I shook myself. *Get it together, Cora.* I had my own life to live, things to do before school started.

Such as? That foolish part of me dared to come up with anything as imperative as following Dorian home.

If I felt like this now, what would I feel like in a month? A year? He would wear away everything I used to care about until all I wanted was to please him.

There had to be some escape.

I looked around the sparkling apartment. I'd planned to clean it because Lisette had been taking up my slack for the last two months. It was time for me to pull my own weight.

But Dorian had already taken care of that.

I washed up, got properly dressed, took out what little trash there was, including my shredded panties, which did little to help me in my goal of not obsessing over Dorian.

Restlessly, I went downstairs to the mailboxes. In the half-lit lobby, I sorted my mail over the trash can— six credit card offers, a shiny grad school brochure, and yet another medical bill, this one with *OVERDUE* stamped on the outside. And, last, an envelope from the University of Chicago.

A thick envelope.

My hands shaking, I tore it open and scanned the contents:

Dear Cora Shaw…. Thank you for your application…. It is with pleasure that we announce your acceptance into the Master of Science program in the Department of Economics at the University of Chicago.

My whoop split the silent air, my heart pounding with joy and relief. I'd been so sick that I'd hardly managed to fill out my application, but I'd managed to drag myself through it with Lisette's help.

Chicago. My top choice, one of the most innovative and exclusive economics programs in the entire country.

I read the letter again, and then a third time, making sure that I hadn't misunderstood. There was no doubt. I really was accepted.

My life had been derailed by cancer, all the plans I'd laid out meaningless in the face of my diagnosis. It was only mule-headed stubbornness that had made me apply to graduate school at all. But now I was cured—

and I'd secured admission into my dream school.

The same school Geoff had been accepted to.

I had a sudden wish that I could call my Gramma and tell her that it had all turned out all right, that I was going to get everything she'd wished that she could give me. That all she'd done was worth it. Everything that had been taken away from me was in my grasp again.

Or at least it would be—if it weren't for the bond that kept me tied to Dorian.

My stomach dropped as I remembered the conversation I'd had with him just an hour before. I was Dorian's cognate. He might indulge my whims as long as I stayed close to him, but that was as far as his tolerance went.

I looked at the letter again and the fat enrollment packet behind it, and my victory turned bitter in my mouth. I now had a door open to everything I had ever wanted. And it was still as impossible for me as it had been when I was dying.

Slowly, I went back to the elevator. It opened at my touch, and I stared at the steel doors as it carried me up, back to my apartment.

I'd won against the cancer, but at the cost of all my goals.

Back in my dorm room, I put on my headset and tapped over to my favorite phone numbers to call Lisette. Dorian hadn't taken my friendship with her away from me. At least, not yet.

But no sooner had I gotten to the screen of favorite contacts than I frowned. There at the top was a new one—"<3 Clarissa." I remembered a random snatch of

Dorian's conversation, something about the djinn being interrogated by Clarissa....

I blinked at the phone. She'd picked it up when I'd dropped it, then, and she'd sent it back...with her phone number as some sort of cute joke?

Gah. It didn't matter. She was the last person I wanted to talk to right then. I tapped Lisette's name decisively.

"So, what have you been up to?" she asked finally after she'd spent an hour detailing her post-Christmas activities with the various member of the Bonner clan.

"Just making sure the apartment's clean." Not quite a lie.

"What, you've been cleaning since Christmas?" she asked skeptically.

"Ha, ha. I went to see the oncologist on Friday," I said, dodging her question and deliberately leaving out my visit to the Health Center to get a birth control prescription. "I should be able to check my results tomorrow."

"Awesome," Lisette said. "I hope the news is good."

"I think I'm feeling too good for it not to be." I took a deep breath. "And you know that CEO I was talking about?"

"Uh-huh." Lisette sounded deeply unimpressed.

"Well, he kind of asked me out last night." I cringed, waiting for her response.

She was incredulous. "You didn't go, though, did you?"

"Maybe I did."

"Cora, what the heck is wrong with you?" she demanded. "How old is this guy? Thirty? Forty?"

"I don't know his exact age, but he doesn't look a day over twenty-five," I said, leaning against the wall. I winced a little at my own reply. It was both honest and outrageously disingenuous.

"I just don't think it's a good idea," Lisette said. "He's probably just using you. I mean, you're young, you're hot, you're grateful...."

"I don't think it's like that," I said.

I could almost hear her eye-roll. "So did he try to get you in bed?"

"Lisette!" I said. There was no way in hell I was answering that. "I think he's going for something more serious than a quick screw."

"Like, how serious?" Again, her voice dripped with suspicion.

I pushed away from the wall and began pacing the room. "Like he gave me a necklace that's worth more than my car."

"And you took it?" Now she was exasperated.

"Sort of," I said. The pendant was still in my pocket, digging slightly into my hip. I didn't know why I'd taken it. "He had it specially made for me. He didn't say so, but he kind of didn't have to."

"Huh," she said dubiously. "And are you ready for something more serious? I mean, you're a senior in college. You've applied for grad school. You have plans."

"Yeah, I know. And I do," I said.

"Well, are you like boyfriend-girlfriend with this

guy?" she asked. "What's his name, anyway? I can't just call him Mr. Moneybags."

"Dorian Thorne. And no, not boyfriend-girlfriend. Not quite." *More like vampire-consort.* Oh, yeah, that would go over well.

"What about Geoff?" she asked.

I felt a pang of guilt, tinged with the slightest hint of panic.

"I don't know," I said.

Again, Geoff. I pushed my hair out of my face. I'd made promises to him, promises that I'd meant. Promises that I still meant? I didn't know. I couldn't think.

"Well, I'm going to hit the Mall in Columbia tomorrow," Lisette said. "Why don't you and Geoff come along?"

I snorted and swept my hair out of my face. "Because Geoff really wants to go clothes shopping with you."

"He'll come to hang out with you, Cora," Lisette said patiently.

"He hasn't called me over break," I said evasively.

"Have you called him?"

"No," I admitted. "We've messaged on Facebook. I told him the therapy's working."

Lisette huffed into the phone. "He's giving you space. Come on, Cora. Before you get in too deep with this Dorian Thorne, you should give Geoff a real try. You actually really know Geoff, and he's a nice guy."

Too deep. Was that before or after Dorian sank his teeth into my throat? Before or after he took what passed for my innocence again and again? I thought of this morning. And again.

"Sure thing," I said aloud.

"Meet you at three? By Marble Slab?"

"Yeah, I'll meet you there."

"Oops. Gotta go," she said. "Mireille wants me to see some new awful viral video."

"Okay," I said. Mireille was Lisette's sister, a freshman in accounting. "See you."

"Bye. Make sure to get our bathroom really clean. I want to see it spotless when I come back."

"Uh-huh." I smiled despite myself. "Nothing keeping you from driving over here and helping out."

"Oh, look, I think I'm having car trouble." She laughed.

"Riiight. Bye," I said.

"Bye."

I hung up and sagged onto the couch. Geoff. I had pretty much made him a promise at the end of the last semester—a promise that I wasn't sure I could keep anymore.

I wasn't even sure I wanted to. And that thought scared me.

As I grabbed some lunch, I realized that the interior of the fridge hadn't been cleaned out. Finally, something to do.

I thought about the problem with Geoff as I scrubbed it, or tried to think about him, anyway, because every time I had his face fixed in my mind's eye, it would blur and Dorian's would replace it—his warm hand on mine replaced by Dorian's cooler, more stirring touch, his mouth with Dorian's kiss. And I thought I could bear that, but far worse was the catalog of Dorian's expressions in my mind's eye, his amusement, his ineffable sadness, and the rare, brief moments of tenderness, as if he were remembering how to feel...

I decided to wash my bedding, and I pulled everything off and shoved it into the washing machine, leaving the door to the laundry closet open so that I could perch on the counter and watch the blankets go round.

My acceptance packet from the University of Chicago sat next to me. I couldn't bear to go through it. Not with the knowledge that I was hardly more likely to attend it now than when I was dying.

I remembered something Dorian had said to me the night before, something about how I'd made those dreams my reason to live. I wouldn't have ever put it that way. I would have just called those things my life, my future. But he was right. They were an idea of a future, not a future itself. And I'd battled my way through classes, though the awful alemtuzumab injections, through everything by repeating to myself the list of all the things I wanted my life to be, all the things that would prove to Gramma that I was happy, successful—that she'd done a good job.

Now that future was more than a dream. It was an actual acceptance letter that I could hold in my hand. Something I'd earned, I'd won myself. Why, then, did Chicago suddenly seem less brilliant next to the image of Dorian's white house?

By the time the sheets and blankets were dry and back on my bed, it was dusk. I flipped on the lights and paced the apartment, hunting vainly for some other spot that Dorian's staff had missed in their cleaning.

Finally, I pulled up Hulu on my laptop and watched the Christmas specials I'd missed as I cleaned out my binders and backpack, making a stack of the books I planned to sell back the next day. I took a shower and curled up in bed with a hot chocolate and my laptop.

And I thought about him. Dorian. Constantly. Obsessively.

Eating lunch, I had thought of him. Folding laundry, my mind was full of him. Throwing out last semester's notes, I couldn't get him out of my head.

It wasn't normal. It wasn't healthy. And I couldn't help it. Knowing that I would see him on Wednesday made me feel far better than it should. If I could just accept this bond—whatever it was—I felt certain that my spinning mind would have some relief, and I could wait until New Year's Eve with some degree of calm. Fighting his claim on me only seemed to make it worse.

But as much as I wanted him, and as much as I missed him, it wasn't enough to get in trade for all of me. Whatever promises he made to not deliberately reshape my mind, I knew he would if it was important enough, and I had a bone-deep conviction that his influence would change me unconsciously no matter what.

It was, as he said, what he was. And what I had become.

But I had my own life. I had my own will, my own direction, my own plans and friends. And I wasn't willing to give them up without a fight.

I woke up early Monday morning to emptiness. An empty apartment, an empty building, an empty campus, an empty life.

I ate breakfast haunted by Dorian's presence. A memory of his voice, his touch, his expression would come over me, and I would freeze in its intensity and the sharp loss of it when it was gone.

I threaded the blood-drop pendant onto one of my own necklaces and put it on. It was a stupid gesture, since I couldn't accept the bond that it represented. But I felt slightly better with it against my skin.

Shaking myself out of my strange fugue, I checked my test results online for my newest lymphocyte count. Fifteen thousand. Still higher than normal, but less than a fifteenth of what it had been at my last test.

I stared the number, stark black on white. It took the last, lingering shadows of doubt away. I truly had been healed.

By him.

Well, then. I guess I really do have to get ready for my last semester of classes.

I washed my bowl, shoved my textbooks in my backpack, and headed to the university bookstore. After dropping my old books off at the sale desk, I headed to the textbooks section, my schedule in my hand.

Using my phone, I crosschecked the store's prices online. It dragged out the entire process into an hour-long ordeal, but it was worth it for the savings. But the total was still too high because I didn't have money for any of it.

I should get another job. I wasn't sick anymore, and the real world came with real costs—ones I couldn't pay right now. I'd had a healthy bank balance after my summer internship, giving me the confidence to agree to move out of the dorms and into the campus apartment with Lisette, Christina, and Chelsea. But I'd counted on being able to keep my work-study gig and the front-desk job with a local moving truck rental franchise.

Neither of those had panned out. Just one week into the semester, I'd been so tired I'd had to give up the rental company job, and a month later, I couldn't keep up the work-study. Rent, food, car insurance, and my cell phone bill had destroyed my summer savings, and I had fifteen hundred dollars of unpaid out-of-pocket health expenses.

I was trying very hard not to raid the very small balance left in my Gramma's bank account. Until her house sold, I needed to pay utilities and taxes on it. But unless I got a job—and fast—I didn't see how else I'd get through the next semester.

Dorian will give you all the money you need, a small voice whispered.

I didn't listen to it.

I finished my online purchases, wincing at the balance. I took the two books I was buying in the store and headed to the checkout. Those would almost be covered by the credit I got from selling my old books back, at least. I'd also have to go to the print shop for the professor-produced materials for art history. On credit, but I'd deal with that later.

I took my receipt and shoved the new books into my backpack, pulling up the hood of my jacket to shade my face. As I lowered my sunglasses and stepped out of the bookstore, a voice called my name.

"Ciao, Cora!"

I turned around to see a familiar face behind a broad pair of Louis Vuitton sunglasses.

"Cosimo?" I asked incredulously. "What are you doing here?"

CHAPTER THIRTEEN

"Spying." Cosimo dropped his voice conspiratorially. "I heard that Dorian's new consort was an actual honest-to-goodness college student, and I had to see for myself. I heard he even lets you live in the dorms. For most consorts, school would be traded in for a Maserati and diamond studs in three days flat."

I had met him when he'd grabbed my arm as I was trying to run from the ballroom during the introduction. Why was he hunting me down here, on campus?

"Maybe I'm different." I narrowed my eyes at him behind my concealing shades. How fast could Dorian get here if I called?

As if he could read my mind, Cosimo said, "Don't worry, *cara*. There's no reason to be afraid." He waggled his fingers in a dismissive motion. "We'll have you back safe and sound in no time."

"Back from where?" I demanded as a low-slung car in a violent yellow rolled up to the curb.

Cosimo opened the rear passenger door. "If you don't get in, you'll never find out. Don't worry. I'm not going to touch a hair on your pretty head. That's very bad form, you know. We're just going on a little field trip. Very educational. If you want to."

"If?" I asked. I looked around. There were at least a dozen people within view on the sidewalk—all human. They couldn't save me from Cosimo. The only thing screaming would do would be to put them in danger, too. If I had a choice, it was because Cosimo was giving it to me.

"Yes, if." He gave me a dazzling smile. "I really mean it. You can stand right here, in your own little world, and never see anything that Dorian doesn't want you to until it's far too late for you to care. Or you can come with me, and I'll show you a few things I'm certain he doesn't want you to know about—and tell you some things that *you* will."

"Why?" I demanded. "Why would I want to know? It's not like I can do anything about anything, one way or another."

He smiled again, showing too many teeth. "What if I told you that you could?"

I caught my breath. Could he mean it?

"In, then, *bella,*" he said, waving. "This is your only chance. In thirty seconds I leave, with you or without you."

I hesitated. Could I trust him? He wasn't doing

something nice because he was my friend, so that left only one other possibility. He planned to do something Dorian didn't want in order to hurt him. Which meant that getting in would betray what Dorian and I shared.

Whatever it was.

"Twenty-five."

Of course, the best way of hurting Dorian would be to take away his cognate. If Cosimo wanted to kill me, though, he wouldn't bother to ask me to get in the car at all. It wasn't like I had the strength to fight off an agnate, nor would anyone else come to help.

"Twenty."

So that meant Cosimo wanted to convince me of something, not kill me outright. And it had to have something to do with the bond.

That thought sent a tremor of unease through me, and then a second spike of fear that I could feel anything but happiness at the thought of doing something to the bond that held me to Dorian.

"Fifteen."

What did I owe Dorian, after all? Sure, he'd saved my life, but only because he wanted it for himself.

I'd never wanted this. I had to be free.

I took off my backpack and got in.

"Excellent!" Cosimo stood in the door and held out his hand. "Your phone, *cara*. Not that I don't adore Dorian's company. It's just that he's not going to be very happy with what I want to show you. If he's tracking you and you come anywhere near where we're going…well, that's an establishment he'd do a great deal to keep you out of."

Reluctantly, I handed him my phone, and he passed it to a woman who had been leaning against the bookstore's brick wall. I'd hardly even noticed her before, but she must be one of Cosimo's thralls. My lifeline to Dorian, my phone with the tracking software he had loaded on it, was now gone.

If I'd been terrified, then maybe Dorian could have sensed it and come to find me, one way or another. But I wasn't. I knew Cosimo was up to no good, but I really did believe that he didn't plan to hurt me, at least directly. If he wanted me dead, there was no reason that I wouldn't be already.

"She'll keep it safe until you come back," Cosimo said, bending down to smile at me through the open door. "Cross my heart. Now, scoot." He made a small waving motion with his hands.

I slid across the bench seat to the other side, and he got in to sit beside me. My skin prickled with uneasiness at his closeness. Just because I trusted him not to kill me didn't mean that I liked him.

"Drive," he said to the chauffeur, and the car began to move.

"Where are we going?" I asked.

"Just a little field trip to Baltimore," he said, pulling his sunglasses off and folding them primly before sliding them into the pocket of his blazer.

Baltimore. Dorian had gone there when I'd been attacked to try to find out who was behind it because the city was a stronghold of the Kyrioi.

That didn't bode well.

"Look, if anything happens to me, Dorian's going

to find out," I said.

Cosimo smiled. "You're welcome to tell him. But I don't think you will."

"Are you going to stop me, then?" I challenged as the car merged onto the Beltway.

"Not at all," he said soothingly. "You'll be free to tell him anything. I'm willing to gamble that you won't want to, though. You're a cognate who immediately leaves her agnate's mansion for school and a dorm room."

"So?"

"So you might be the kind of cognate who would jump at a way out. Out of everything. No more blood. No more sex. No more bond."

My heart began to hammer in my chest. I hardly dared to believe it. "That's not possible."

"Has Dorian told you that?"

I ran through every conversation I'd had with him, and I realized that he hadn't. Not in so many words. He'd told me how bonds couldn't be broken—but not that they couldn't be broken at all.

"Can you break a bond?" I pressed.

"Me? Not at all," he said. "Agnates can't break bonds. Just trying it would kill me as surely as it would you, and I'm not suicidal. But they can be broken."

"How?"

"That little nugget will wait until the end of our field trip. Just think of it as an incentive. Go along, take the tour, get a good long look at what you're getting yourself into—and then you'll be able to make an informed decision."

He was enjoying this. I could see it on his face. I opened my mouth to argue, but I decided I didn't want to give him the satisfaction, so I shut it again and settled into the car seat, pulling off my shades.

I watched Cosimo narrowly, but he ignored me, poking at his phone as we drove north.

Dorian would look for me if I were scared enough. But now curiosity was uppermost. Was there really some way to weaken or even escape the obligations of the bond?

We took the Baltimore-Washington Parkway up to the loop and then took an exit into the city. I tensed slightly in my seat. It was the bad part of town—hell, most of the city proper was the bad part of town, but this was bad even for B'more.

The car turned, then turned again. Ugly rowhouses crowded block after block up against the cracked sidewalks, a concrete jungle of red brick and blank windows, half of them shattered or boarded up and tagged with layered graffiti. The sun glared onto acres of asphalt and cement, the only relief the weeds that pushed up through cracks in the sidewalk and in the dirt that collected against the houses. I glimpsed a single tree as we drove by—through the front window of a shell of a house, the roof and floors above having long ago fallen into the earthen basement.

Though the houses looked derelict, the streets buzzed with tense activity. Teenagers lounged on the corners, sharp eyes fixed on our car as it passed. Men sat on stoops, smoking and drinking, their dogs chained to the metal railings. They called out to the clutches of people who prowled the streets with catcalls and insults that I could hear through the closed windows, some friendly, others not.

Great. We were driving straight through a scene from *The Wire*.

"Why are we here?" I demanded, an ugly suspicion forming in my mind. Cosimo had said he would not touch a hair on my head, but if he left me in a place like this, he wouldn't have to.

"I want you to see our world," he said. "All of it. Dorian keeps you locked up in that house like the princess on the glass mountain. He doesn't want you to know what it's really like."

There was a break between two blocks of row houses, forming a narrow alley that faded into the shadows. The driver turned down it and was flagged to a stop by a man with the blunt end of a pistol sticking out of his waistband.

The driver rolled down the window. Somewhere, a child started to cry, and a woman's sharp voice ordered it to be quiet.

"What d'you want?" the man on the street asked roughly.

"We belong here," Cosimo called, and I felt the wave of influence pour out from him.

The man settled back. "Right, then."

The car rolled on.

Behind the block of houses, the alley ended in a tall chain link fence that blocked the way into the bleak expanse of an abandoned brownfield. The man walked over to the gate as the car idled, pushing it open. The car rolled in across the cracked, overgrown road.

Rusting hulks of metal were scattered across the property, tangles of scrubby trees growing out among them. Wide squares of broken concrete formed a checkerboard amid the weeds and grasses and led to the skeleton of a manufacturing plant, its smokestacks punching up into the gray sky. The lot ended at the banks of the brown river.

"There's nothing here," I said, my stomach tightening.

"Oh, but there is, Cora Shaw," Cosimo said. "It's many things to many people. But for you, it's a chance to get to know our world away from Dorian's watchful eye."

The car continued across the broken patchwork of concrete and asphalt, moving closer to the old factory. A prickle of unease came over me as we approached. It was the only possible destination here.

The car went around the corner of the building, and abruptly, we were facing a pad of clean white concrete, the parking spaces marked with freshly painted yellow lines. Dozens of cars were there, hidden from the view of both the river and the gate by two arms of the abandoned factory.

Not abandoned, then. Not at all.

The driver pulled into a parking space and turned off the car. Cosimo opened his door. I could hear the thud of bass coming from the building.

"Of course, today, there will be no one here of importance," Cosimo said conversationally as he circled the car. "I asked around. Better not to come to the attention of some—yes, even I hesitate at that. Does it surprise you?"

I didn't say anything as I shoved my sunglasses on, but he hardly paused as he opened my door.

"We're here for the atmosphere, Cora, not the politics. And that will be quite enough."

I didn't see that I had a choice. Cosimo's friend still had my phone. And somehow, I did believe him now, that he didn't plan to hurt me. At least at the moment.

I got out of the car, leaving my backpack on the floor and ignoring the arm that Cosimo offered me with exaggerated gallantry.

"Oh, a modern girl," he said. "Doesn't hold truck with any of the conventions of the past. I like that."

"Or maybe I just don't like you," I said.

Cosimo laughed as if I'd just told an excellent joke. "Of course! But let's not hang around out here. There are so many people who are eager to meet you, or at least they would be if they knew you were coming. And all this sunlight isn't good for my complexion."

"I've met them already at the introduction," I said, but I followed him toward a narrow steel door set in the crumbling brick.

"Oh, no," Cosimo said. "You've only met the vampires."

I stopped in my tracks. Only the vampires. That meant I could expect djinn inside the building. Djinn—and maybe other things.

Cosimo looked back, his eyes hidden behind the glasses as he smiled disarmingly. "Coming, *bella*?"

Right.

I strode forward, brushing past him, and knocked loudly on the steel door.

Nothing happened.

"Very impressive," Cosimo said, "if ineffective."

He reached past me, rapping out a fast rhythm on the door.

I looked askance. "A secret knock? Really?"

He smiled. "It works."

The door opened so suddenly that I had to jump back to keep from being struck by it. A massive head stuck out, covered in golden scales, and I swallowed a scream.

CHAPTER FOURTEEN

Adjinn in its natural form. But—I realized almost instantly—not the same djinn that had attacked me a few days before. Where the other one had been fast and lean, this one was heavy, muscle-bound, even. And its features were definitely male.

It looked me up and down, then turned to Cosimo.

"No food and drink from outside," the djinn snapped, blinking its yellow eyes from behind its heavy black-rimmed glasses. Its voice was a surprising light tenor.

"She's a cognate," Cosimo said.

The djinn turned back to me. The black slits of its nostrils flared. "She doesn't smell like a cognate."

"She's fresh. Converted in the last two weeks," Cosimo said patiently.

"If you're feeding me a load of crap, Mortensen

will have something to say about it," the djinn said.

Cosimo held up his hands, palms out. "He was at her introduction himself two nights ago. It's good."

The djinn's eyes narrowed. "She's *that* cognate, then. And she's coming here? With you?"

"Mind your own business and let us in," Cosimo said.

"It's your funeral," the djinn said, but he pushed the door all the way open so that Cosimo could catch it.

"After you," Cosimo said, waving me inside.

I stepped inside the narrow corridor, edging past the djinn who stood against the wall with his arms folded over his chest. Despite my nerves, I had a moment of bemusement when I realized that it was wearing a Fringe Festival t-shirt and artfully aged jeans.

A hipster djinn. Well, why not?

An old-style TV blared *Judge Judy* in a small room off to the side across from a stained, overstuffed leather couch. I stopped to pull off my sunglasses and shoved them into the pocket of my jacket. Cosimo passed me, continuing down the narrow, dingy hall.

"Coming, *cara?*" His voice floated back over pounding bass.

"Of course," I said, falling in step behind him.

A cat paced ahead of us, its tail an exclamation mark as it picked delicately across the stained concrete floor. I regarded it suspiciously, but it seemed to be just that—an ordinary fat tabby.

Dirty, unmarked doors interrupted the painted cinderblock at intervals. Cosimo ignored them, heading for the black drape that hung across the end of the hall. I looked back in time to see the djinn disappear into the TV room.

I wondered if it watched *Judge Judy* ironically.

We reached the heavy drape at the end of the corridor. The pounding bass was louder now, coming from beyond it. Cosimo pushed it aside as he stepped through, and I ducked through behind him with the cat twining around my legs.

And I gaped.

The factory floor was one great room with red brick and cinderblock walls extending up at least thirty feet. The old glass block windows, high up in the walls, were so grimed with old dirt that only the palest light filtered down, and a maze of catwalks, scaffolds, and platforms formed a tangle of iron and wood against the long walls.

But it wasn't the room that made my blood freeze in my veins. It was the clientele. And though the room was more than half-empty at this early hour, it only served to highlight their weirdness.

My gaze was first arrested by the movement on the dance floor at the center of the tables, where two couples stood ringed by knots of observers. They all looked human…at first glance, though between their hairstyles and body modifications, the crowd would fit right into a punk-horror show.

I didn't have to be told that none of them were actually human at all.

Each couple moved together as one, their steps synchronized with the throbbing music. One woman's tattoos crawled across her back and arms, up her neck and across her face, and her partner sported several pounds of metal in his face. Their audience wore cheek plugs and horn implants, piercings tied with ribbon like corsets, puckered scars cut in patterns across bare skin, and angry, half-healed burns.

"What have they done to themselves?" I didn't realized I'd spoken aloud until I heard the words.

"Don't worry," Cosimo said lightly. "Among aethers, accelerated healing is one of the most common traits. A tattoo, a piercing—for most races, it will last only a few weeks, at most a couple of months. Think of it like a costume or even a pair of particularly uncomfortable heels."

Which meant that they had to do those things to themselves over and over to maintain such a look. My stomach lurched. I wasn't sure if Cosimo had meant to reassure me, but if he had, he'd failed.

I watched the dancing couples, unable to look away. The movements of one pair were simple, little more than keeping time. But the other....

It was hard to know if they were dancing or trying to kill each other. The male held the female by the back of the neck, taking slow, angry steps forward as she moved back with him. There was a flash of motion, almost too fast to follow, and suddenly she was tumbling across the floor, thrown by a furious gesture.

I gasped involuntarily even as their audience cheered. But her fall was graceful, the rolls as elegant as they were angry, and she came to rest in a half-split with one leg out behind her, her face turned down and arm extended, demanding. The man strode up to her, took her hand—and she flew through the air, rolling across his back with her legs sharply scissored, and then her feet were on the ground and the male was the one flying, thrown over her shoulders and onto the floor. She turned in time to the music and slapped him hard, twice, the sound of the contact sharp enough to ring out over the thudding of the music.

"Not as pretty as the Lesser Introduction, is it?" Cosimo remarked. "Dancing. It's one of the oldest forms of expression. Listen to what we want to say when we're amongst ourselves and not on our best behavior."

The audience was hooting with enthusiasm, and the man caught his partner's wrist in the middle of a violent movement and slammed her body into his, beginning a slow, steady step as the other couple began their own lyrical altercation.

But they hadn't gotten far when the male hit the ground hard—too hard. The audience made a sound like a kind of sigh as he pushed up with one hand, the other hanging from his arm at a sickening angle. He stared at it for a long moment, his partner standing a short distance away and panting while the first couple stopped to watch. Then he gave a laugh, high and sharp, straightening the broken hand with the other and then letting it flop unnaturally again. He laughed again, louder.

There was some muttering in the group, and several of the observers went onto the floor—to help, I thought at first. But they grabbed him roughly by the shoulders and began hauling him away. He stopped laughing abruptly, and he balled up his good hand into a fist and plowed it into the nearest jaw.

The dance floor erupted in chaos—the impossible speed of the agnates, the sudden flash of djinns' golden scales, a streak of furry animal bodies, and other things my brain couldn't even put a name to.

Around the perimeter of the dance floor, the nearest patrons stood up leisurely and moved back to tables closer to the walls. But the rest of the clientele watched with incurious eyes as the brawl continued, the bartenders behind the shiny copper bar doing little more than glancing up before returning to their work.

"What the hell is that about?" I demanded, wheeling around to face Cosimo.

"Ah, the exhib. Exhibition dancing—a combination of capoeira, danse apache, dirty swing, and various street styles," he said easily. "It's very popular. Earlier incarnations have been around for centuries. This is what we're like when you're not around, Cora. When we don't put on our pretty clothes and wipe our faces clean of all the things that might upset you."

"Dorian isn't like that," I said.

"That's because Dorian was dying," Cosimo snapped. "Inch by inch, year by year, he was dying, *cara*. We agnates don't get old and we don't get sick. We just shut down. Dorian didn't come here only because he couldn't feel enough for it to make a difference anymore."

"He doesn't seem to be dying to me," I said, his words making a heavy, angry knot in the pit of my stomach.

"Because he has you." He lifted a hand to brush against my cheek, and I shied away. "He's a vampire—a parasite. He feeds on your life. Without a cognate, don't think he'd be too damn noble to find life on his own, like these people are."

"Like the rushers you left me next to during the introduction," I said.

"That was very naughty of me," Cosimo admitted. "But I knew that if Dorian got his way, he'd hide all the unpretty parts of our society away from you until it was too late."

"It's already too late," I said.

"It's close, *cara*. Too close. Once he has his hooks in you good and solid—and don't pay any attention to what he says, because he will get his hooks in, just as we all do—you won't even consider dissolving the bond and returning to your old life. But right now, perhaps, it still has some attraction for you."

Like Geoff and the University of Chicago....

The brawl was subsiding, some fighters slinking away, others being dragged by friends or enemies away from the dance floor.

"So you're bringing me here...to scare me straight? Like some kind of anti-drug program, but with vampires?"

He laughed then, a bright sound in the dark room. "Brilliant! I wish I'd found you before Dorian did. You're wasted on him."

"You wouldn't give me that choice, though, would you?"

He cocked his head. "Why would you assume

that?"

"You're a Kyrioi. You have to be."

Now there were only three figures left on the dance floor, a djinn and a vampire pummeling an unconscious form on the floor. I tried not to look at them.

If anything, Cosimo looked more amused. "What does that have to do with anything?"

"Kyrioi don't respect humans," I said stiffly.

The last two fighters finally tired of their attack and stepped away, leaving a broken body sprawled at the edge of the dance floor.

"But you're not human," Cosimo pointed out. "At least not any more. And what would be the fun of that? You're much more adorable as a spitfire."

"So Etienne and Isabella—"

He cut me off, shuddering. "Disgusting. A blow-up doll with blood."

Good and evil. Black and white. It was already muddled in Dorian's world, and now it seemed that all the colors were running together.

I couldn't think straight. The Kyrioi were Dorian's enemy. They despised humans. But Cosimo, for all his contempt, seemed more humane than some of Dorian's allies.

"May I buy you a drink?" he said then.

"Do they have anything here that won't kill me?" I asked, eyeing the bar suspiciously.

He snorted. "There's not much that would, here. We aethers are remarkably derivative in our tastes."

"Aethers?" I echoed. It was the second time he'd used that word.

"Nonhumans," he said. "Or, more correctly, super-humans. Agnates. Djinn. Shifters. Elves. Faes, in all their variety."

"Okay," I said, filing away that list for later consideration.

"Anyhow, Mortensen stocks just about anything you could desire—not just booze," he continued, stepping up to the bar between two other customers. "The Plant is an unconventional institution for an unconventional clientele. Care for a latte? Juice?"

I decided to take a gamble. After all, if he wanted to kill me, he didn't need to use poison to do it. "You can buy me a chai."

He signaled to the nearest bartender, and the man stepped over. No, not a human man, I realized as I joined him, and not an agnate or a djinn either. His face had an almond-eyed beauty to that was almost feminine, and a peculiar, almost blue cast to his skin. I blinked, and he looked ordinary again.

"A peppermint white chocolate mocha, double whipped cream for me," he said. "And for my friend, a chai—and a banana pecan muffin, because she's looking peaky."

Wordlessly, the bartender busied himself at a coffee station a short distance away.

"Take a good look around," Cosimo said. "You're still human enough that you might not be able to see everyone as they properly are, but you should be able to see more than an ordinary human can. Take a good, hard look."

I did, noticing for the first time the tables hidden

away under the catwalks, booths with high walls between them. The figures there sat in groups of two to four, never next to one another, heads bent close as they whispered. And I noticed too how everyone else in the room carefully avoided looking their way.

The power brokers. Not human, because no humans were allowed here. Because the real power wasn't in human hands at all....

I turned my attention to the man perched on a stool next to Cosimo. At first, I was afraid he'd find my attention rude, but he didn't seem to notice it any more than he had the fight on the dance floor. I stared until my eyes watered, and for a long time, he looked just like a man, ordinary silver-shot brown hair and a middle-aged face with a nose like a lumpy potato. There was nothing that was the least bit unusual about him.

I was about to give up when he turned slightly and my vision...shifted. I had the sensation that he hadn't turned a different portion of his body toward me so much as rearranged the part that I could see. I pushed away from the bar, and keeping my eyes fixed on him, I stepped carefully in a wide half-circle around him.

Again I had that sensation, like the part of him I was seeing was being created for my view as I looked at it. And I had the sense that the other parts of him, the parts that I couldn't see, were simply...not there.

And still the man didn't give the least impression of noticing me.

"You can see it, then, can't you?" Cosimo asked.

I pulled my gaze away from him with difficulty and looked past him to where Cosimo still stood at the bar.

"You're on the other side. What do you see?"

"The same as you. It affects everyone the same." He shrugged. "As far as I know, they've never spoken to anyone. They don't eat. They don't sleep. They mostly live among the homeless in the streets, but sometimes they come in here and sit."

"But why?" My gaze was dragged back to the man. He sat with his chin in his hand, blinking slowly at nothing.

"No one knows. No one is even sure they're alive. Some people think they're a projection or a program of some sort. But I will tell you one thing—don't touch them. They don't like it. Those who have survived say that when you touch them, you can sometimes feel…nothing. The parts that you can't see just aren't there."

Carefully, I circled back around again to stand by Cosimo. Compared to that thing, even he felt safe.

The bartender set two tall white porcelain mugs in front of us, plus a small plate with a fat muffin next to mine. A tower of whipped cream stood above the rim of Cosimo's absurd confection.

Cosimo took a deep drink of his coffee and made a noise of appreciation, licking the cream from his lips.

"What will those humans think of next?" he said, holding up the cup.

But I wasn't thirsty anymore—because when I looked around the room, my shifted vision remained.

Two women appeared to be sitting at one table with an appetizer sampler between them. To ordinary vision, they appeared to be eating—or at least, they appeared to have eaten, because the food was disappearing, and there was the impression in my mind that this had happened because they ate it. But when I looked closely, I could see some kind of shadowy shape that joined them, like a thick black rope, and the food that was disappearing was being torn with rhythmical motions into tiny pieces that then were simply absorbed.

A movement under one of the catwalks pulled away my horrified gaze. A man was standing there—or had been standing there, because suddenly his face shifted, dissolved into iridescence, and a flurry of butterflies exploded from it, leaving a hole behind as they circled quickly around his disintegrating head and then settled back again, rearranging his features into another shape.

The fat tabby cat slunk up beside him and lunged at a stray butterfly, catching it out of the air. The insect seemed to writhe, the body swelling in the cat's mouth as the wings shrunk down into itself, and the man stooped with a fluid motion and caught the cat by the nape of the neck, giving it a sharp shake until the surprised feline dropped the erstwhile butterfly with a yowl.

The insect flopped on the ground for a moment like a black grub, but the man bent to scoop it up—and it seemed to slip into his fingers and was gone.

"You think you know the world?" Cosimo said softly. "You don't even know the beginning. All the old stories, the fairytales and the legends, they all have a kernel of truth. But the reality is far darker than you can imagine. Do you think that vampires are the stuff of nightmares? Compared to most of the fae, we're a happy bedtime story."

I turned back to face him. "What's all this supposed to accomplish?"

"I'm trying to show you that even after every shock, every horror that you've experienced so far, you don't know the first thing about our world," he said. "You don't know what kind of life Dorian is inviting you to join. And you have no idea how much it will cost you."

I pushed away from the bar, leaving my chai and my muffin untasted. "Okay. I came. I saw. Take me home now."

Cosimo lifted one shoulder in a half-shrug. "As you wish."

He finished his mocha confection in one more swallow and left a folded twenty on the counter, then led the way back through the curtain without another word.

I didn't speak until the car was going back through the chain link gates.

"So tell me now. You've been hinting at it since you picked me up. How do you break a bond?"

"I don't," he said. "But you can."

Tell me. My heart was so loud that I could hardly hear the words.

"Unfaithfulness," he said succinctly. "If you know another human man—in the biblical sense—then the bond is shattered. Forever. It can never be restored. You go back to being human, and you live your life as if nothing had ever happened."

"And the cancer?" I pressed. I felt lightheaded

Could it be that easy?

"Pardon?" he asked.

"I had cancer when I was...changed. Bonded. Whatever. Would it come back?" I had to know.

"Those sorts of things are healed at conversion. They don't magically reappear if you go back to being human. A cognate who is three hundred years old doesn't suddenly dry up and turn into dust, either. You simply revert and pick up living as a human where your body is now." He shrugged negligently. "That doesn't mean you can't get a new cancer later. Human is human. You could die of kidney failure or a heart attack, too."

Gone forever, he'd said. "And if Dorian...bites me again?"

Cosimo's answer was simple. "You both die."

"If I'm human, then Dorian will look for another cognate."

"Well, yes, that is pretty much the point," Cosimo said condescendingly. "When the bond is broken, you no longer have a bond."

"More women will die, then." How could I damn them to that? That was my hesitation, surely. I wasn't thinking about what those other women might do under Dorian's mouth, in Dorian's bed. Those thoughts were too dangerous to entertain.

Cosimo's laugh was mocking. "Altruism can only take you so far, and if you aren't interested in what Dorian has to offer.... Well, you know yourself that there are reasons someone like you would gamble her life for a vampire's kiss. Sure, you might be sparing some...more hurried deaths by staying bonded to Dorian, but you might also be keeping another girl from being saved like you were."

"But I would lose him." I didn't realize I was going to say those words until they had already escaped.

God, that thought hurt. I knew that no one could ever make me feel the way he did. Make me want the way he did. Need the way he did. But why did that thought hurt...like that?

It wasn't just lust. Even if I decided breaking the bond was what I wanted, I knew I'd wound him deeply with my betrayal, and that hurt, too, which was the craziest and scariest thing of all.

But how could I betray him by breaking a bond I'd never agreed to? And how could I keep the bond, keep him, when it meant I'd have to lose not only everything I'd ever wanted but my very self? How could I even want to?

"Do you really want him?" Cosimo asked. "That's what you have to ask yourself. Do you really want him? Or is it just the bond? Does he just want you to want him?"

I sat in silence for a long moment. My life had seemed to be closing in around me, shuttling me down a single pathway to my destiny even as I fought against it. Now I had a choice. I had thought I would do anything to escape the road that I had been set upon.

Now I wasn't so sure.

If I took the path back to humanity, there was no going back. Perhaps all my cravings were just the bond or Dorian's twisting of my mind or both. In that case, I could shake them off once I was out from under his power, and I would consider myself lucky to have escaped such a dark fate.

But if they were not, then what we had was real, and I would be left holding nothing but a handful of regrets.

Was any of this even true? I didn't know why Cosimo would lie, other than that he was a Kyrioi, but I didn't know why he might tell me the truth, either.

"You're only telling me this to hurt him," I said.

"Oh, most definitely," Cosimo agreed.

But if he really was helping me, should I care?

"I have no way of knowing that it's true. Having sex with a human could end up killing me, for all I know. It would be a pretty good trick, getting me to kill myself after the djinn the Kyrioi sent after me failed."

He held up a finger. "First of all, the Kyrioi are no more a single group than the Adelphoi are. And I had nothing to do with the djinn."

I looked at him narrowly. "But you know who did."

He shrugged. "The secrets of others aren't mine to share. No, what I want is Dorian's humiliation. I want clear proof that the world he presents is not and never can be real."

"Through me," I said.

"You're already his tool. His symbol," Cosimo said. "What would be better to use against him?"

Maybe I really could be human again, free from Dorian and his impossible demands and control. As frightening as he was, I believed that he wouldn't hurt me if I broke the bond. I could have a regular life. No more sunglasses and hoods. I could go to grad school. Date Geoff. I could have a real family. I'd grow old and die, but it would be after a life full of all the things I'd ever wanted.

If this was true, Dorian had hidden it from me deliberately, just as he'd hidden the fact that he expected me to have his children.

The car pulled up to the curb in front of the bookstore, where the woman Cosimo had given the phone to still stood, waiting. Cosimo got out and held out his hand to her.

"Thank you, *cara*," he said with his most charming smile.

The woman blinked, then handed over the phone. She seemed to shake herself slightly, and then she walked away as if she hadn't just been standing for the past two hours in front of a bookstore.

Shoving on my sunglasses, I slid across the bench seat to get out onto the sidewalk. I slung my book bag across my back.

Cosimo handed the phone to me. "Call Dorian. Ask him. See what he says about breaking the bond. I doubt he'll lie to you. It doesn't agree with his philosophy."

No, Dorian wouldn't lie to me. But if he thought it was important enough, he would change me. I knew that now. And I couldn't think of anything more important than this. I would have to confirm it some other way.

"Thank you," I said quietly. "For telling me this. Even though I know you didn't do it for me."

He held out his hand. I didn't take it, and after a moment, he shoved it into his pocket as if nothing had happened and said, "So nice talking to you, Cora. I hope you have a wonderful day. And that you make the choice that is best for *you*."

"I will," I said. *I hope.*

He ducked back into the car. "See you around. Or not."

I watched his car roll away, and I realized that for the first time since I had walked out of Dr. Robeson's office with my terminal diagnosis, I might have a real choice.

There might just be a way out.

The story continues in…

BLOOD BOND

Cora's Choice – Book 5
AETHEREAL BONDS

**Want to read the first chapter right now? Sign
up for the newsletter at AetherealBonds.com
to get exclusive access—for free!
Get free content and release updates.**

The bite of a vampire saved Cora Shaw's life—but
at the price of an eternal bond that gives him complete
power over her mind and body. Dorian Thorne offers
worldly riches, eternal youth, physical pleasure, and even
a kind of happiness. But the vampire had already shown
that he will change even Cora's innermost thoughts
when it suits him, so Cora knows she has everything to
lose.

But Cora discovers that the bond may not be eternal, and she finds herself facing a choice: to break the
bond and resume her old life—or to keep it and choose
Dorian at the risk of losing herself.

The bond, once broken, can never be repaired, so
Cora is playing for keeps with the most important
decision of her life. But each choice comes with its own
terrible price.

About the Author

V. M. Black is the creator of Aethereal Bonds, a sensual paranormal romance urban fantasy series that takes vampires, shifters, and faes where they've never been before. You can find her on AetherealBonds.com. Visit to connect through her mailing list and various social media platforms across the web.

She's a proud geek who lives near Washington, D.C., with her family, and she loves fantasy, romance, science fiction, and historical fiction.

All of her books are available in a number of digital formats. Don't have an e-reader? No problem! You can download free reading apps made by every major retailer from your phone or tablet's app store and carry your books with you wherever you go.

Made in the USA
Lexington, KY
09 November 2014